ENDLESS

I ARRIVED

THE LABORS SERIES
BOOK 1

YUGO VEX

ENDLESS: I ARRIVED

By Yugo Vex

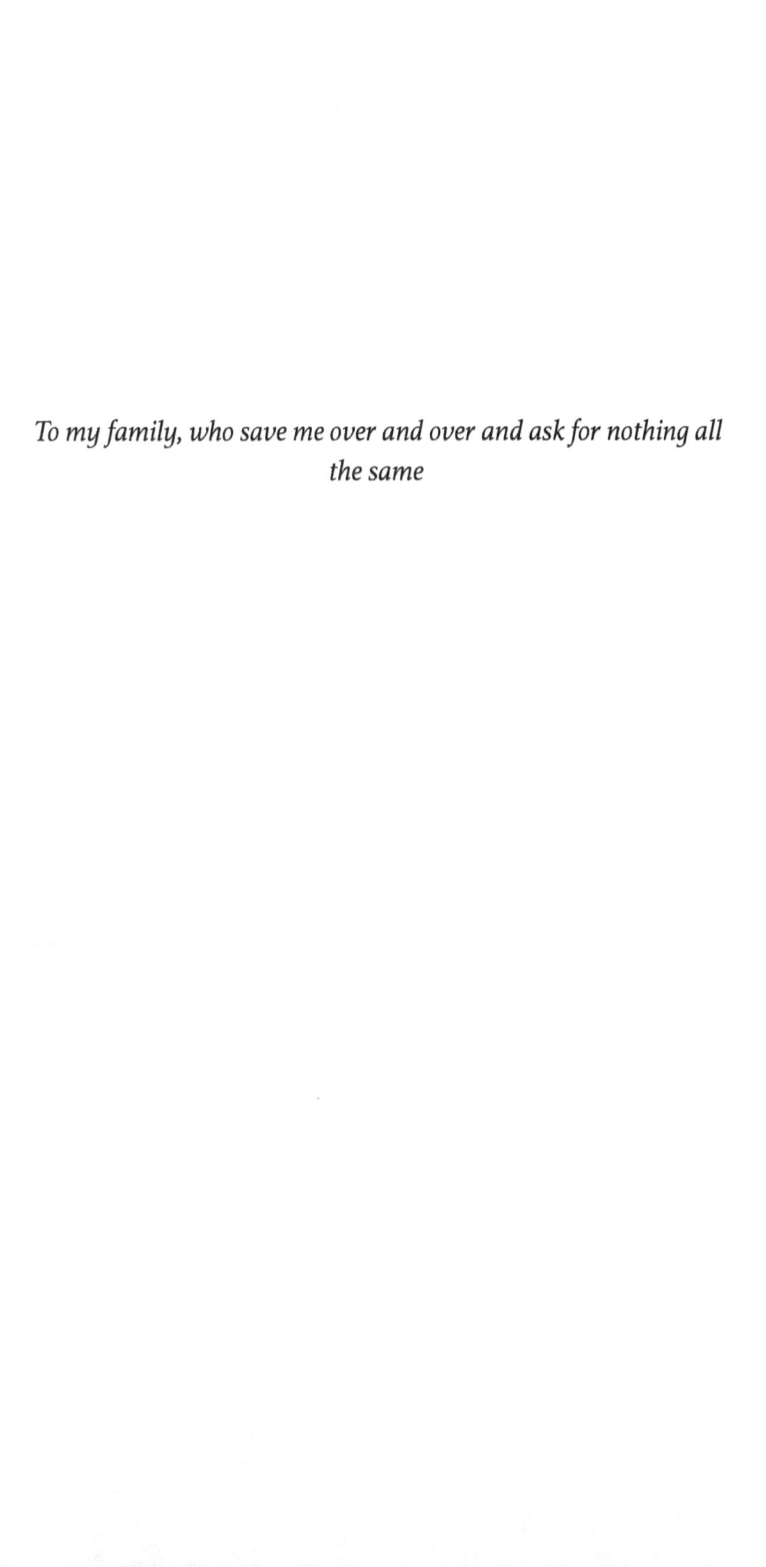

To my family, who save me over and over and ask for nothing all the same

ACKNOWLEDGEMENTS

Edited By Christina Calhoun (@xtinalauren12)
Book Cover Illustration by @Draftsman79
Cover Lettering by Edith Ho (@fl3xdith)

PART 1
1ST REPRIEVE

I ARRIVED AT THE ANSWER. She smiled, "You made it."

Finding 'Else' was not as easy as simply relying on a map. The best way to describe the endeavor was akin to looking through an equation until you managed to find a variable that hadn't been included. The equation here being *where* to navigate through. The variable being Else. Any sign that you were going to a specific *place* meant you were on the mark; it meant you had the equation right in front of you. Eventually, I learned being on the mark didn't mean you were getting any closer to Else, since the variable you thought you could find in the equation might've been the sum's question that you were never given.

Being on track to find where no pathways could lead to proved troublesome and being on the right-track was downright counter-intuitive. Following a route, predetermined or not, only averted your gaze from all of the where not included on your course. And that's where Else lied.

It wasn't a matter of deciding where you should go and it wasn't about locating where not to go either. It was specifically a destination you couldn't pin down to coordinates... Else – where *areas* didn't tend to be.

"What is your name, traveler?" The Answer asks.

She went straight ahead and asked for my name. Those are important for existences (who's exist) like us. But I did travel all the way here to meet who was standing here before me.

"Endless," I reply.

"Oh? And how long did it take you to get here, Endless?"

Does she already know my *expression*?

It took decades of navigating through phantasmic dreadscapes, cataclysmic infernos, and areas I should've never laid eyes on to get to Else. Most of those decades were just spent on me trying to lose the trails, pathways that gave a sign of my position. It was no small task. To start, reaching Else took being off-the-grid of any kind of landmark you could rely on to tell you where you were. I had to abandon all sense of direction as I made my way through incessant locations, searching. This was difficult, given that every active existence – every who – has their own internal compass which guides them in just that, a certain direction when all other means of extrapolating bearing are removed.

Learning to travel without letting instinct determine my course wrought difficulty. To make it to my destination, the journey was one I had to take by moving in a manner between randomly and lost. That was a big first step. Realizing my having bearing itself was an impediment on this expedition, was next. Ridding myself of that came just short of a transformative experience, involving me in an encounter with the *embodiment* Further, who lived up to his namesake.

From there it was a matter of meandering through as many different geographies as it would take before I found Else, some much stranger than others. I'll never forget seeing the edge of space. I had everywhere to get through for one elusive destination to find. Imagine closing your eyes and trying to navigate a maze – that's what the trek felt like. I was lucky enough to stumble upon a few distinct areas which expedited my trip through Where. Otherwise, finding Else could've gone from taking decades to spanning centuries.

"Not long" I reply, relatively speaking.

As an *embodiment* you are your namesake. Take Further; he's always at least one step ahead; for The Answer in front of me, I have yet to see her *expression*, but I already have a hypothesis I want to test; and for me, it means I'm what my namesake so readily reveals; Endless. I have no end, which to put into practical terms means I have no age limit. I'll just carry on existing, or as I like to put it: *keep going*, among other things not relevant to her question.

"Good! Some spend lifetimes trying to get here and still don't," she says gesturing her arm around our current whereabouts. Floating green globules populate our surroundings, clumping when they meet, emitting a brighter glow that illuminates this viscous world.

Once you were in Else, it seemed to behave like it actually had an internal logic to it. It was stable enough to be called 'here', from the inside. All around us, what does not belong to any place drifts, in parallel to the way that Else is not anywhere that could be pinned down to any kind of cartography. Elements untethered by the laws of standard physics spring into view and vanish just as suddenly. Here, one captivates my sight in particular.

The element, no larger than the size of my palm, emanates waves which seem to distend its aerial surroundings as it hovers, creating a mirage effect in the air around it. It pulses almost rhythmically. The Answer lets me stare at the object briefly, before it is gone, taking with it that patch of presence. It leaves an opening in its absence through which I can see the alternating vistas of stars in the vacuum of space, to the amorphous membrane-like lining of a dimensional boundary to the sense-defying sprawl of ethereal planetoids on some trans-existential plane. Just as some of the *locations* begin to bleed in through the opening, the floating gap quickly seals shut, returning that sector of externality to Else's locality.

"Where did it go?" I ask, watching the ripple effect of the element's waves slowly leaving to wherever the matter has translocated.

"Nothing here is tied to any place. What you see in front of you is not yet bound by location-" she says, and as she speaks, what can only be described as a *something*; scaled, larger than either myself or her, in the shape of a darkened grey oval, wider on its almost flat bottom, appears before us. It writhes erratically, the scales of what looks to be its shell separating and rejoining out of tandem. I can't be sure it's an object. I can't be sure if it's alive. It sprouts four appendages from between the scales of the bottom of its shell, perhaps something like an exoskeleton, and lodges them into the ground beside where we stand. It steals our focus for a few seconds, before I try my best to ignore it and get back to my line of questioning.

"You said not yet?" I continue.

"Yes. When the circumstances call for it, however, *places* may naturally be a part of reactions which necessitate the inclusion of some foreign material."

I think I understand what she means, but I stay silent in hope that she might continue.

She notices and smiles again.

"You saw those stars through the wake left behind by that object's departure. They may have undergone a process which led to that specific matter being called to fill the reaction's result. Then again, there were a lot of locations shown through that little breach, so who's to say where the element really went."

I have a feeling she does. Some nagging inclination tells me I need to test out my hypothesis about her expression. That requires more questioning.

"Does that mean these substances begin existing here? Is this where they're created before they're shunted off to different locations?"

"You ask difficult questions."

"Call me inquisitive. I did just get here." Besides, she is *The Answer*. If my hypothesis is correct in coming here, it stands to reason that she'd know.

"That is true." She takes a moment and pauses. Her eyebrows furrow before her eyes light up.

"Reaching here, you must have gathered that Else is no easy destination to pinpoint. It lies where areas don't tend to be. Some areas expand. Take space for example– to remain where areas don't tend to be, Else must be found elsewhere. Or to be more accurate, Else must be found in elsewhere."

I just got that. Areas can be found Where. Or as she would put it: In Where; the map of places, locations, and co-ordinates. Else is different. It's where areas aren't. Elsewhere. And I already know how difficult it is to be where areas weren't. I had given the decades to do it. There's something about how she describes Else though: Where areas don't tend to be. It's near identical to the description of Else I had come to understand during my journey: Where areas didn't tend to be. That can't be a coincidence.

"Many things exist elsewhere, out of cohesion with what exists on some chartable level," she continues. "Being else-where, these things are in a constant state of flux in their lack of defined placement. In a region like elsewhere, where things are situated is not a given."

"And as such, a destination like Else, which is particularly evasive in its whereabouts amongst the contents of elsewhere, acts as a sponge for things drifting through elsewhere to be picked up as the region shifts. It's somewhat of a collector of things that don't belong. Where those things that don't belong come from, is a question for another answer entirely." She giggles.

That makes sense. But there's something about the way she's replying to my questions, using phrases like 'for things that don't belong'; almost exactly how I described the debris floating around us. It's as if she's catering her answers to me in the way I can best understand them. It's uncanny. And it seems like she's having fun with this. I'm sure this has something to do with her...

She interjects before I have a chance to finish my thought: "So how did you know I'd be here?" she questions.

I'm caught off guard.

"I got a tip off," I say, purposefully giving her as little as I can.

"And?"

"And I'll leave it at that."

Some stories were better left untold. For now.

"That's no fun. That's an answer I would like to *Attain* at some point." She says with a wink.

She knows the tip involved my encounter with *Attain*. She's already ascertained her answer. If it was just a hypothesis before, she just tested against my prediction. It proved correct. I'm sure I've figured out her expression – the manifestation of an embodiment's nature as a living concept – now.

"In any case, let me show you around while you're here," she says.

Else, everything areas aren't. As we walk farther away from the position she found me at when I arrived, the malleable oceanic sky begins to work its way down from above, until we are walking through a tunnel of the scenery's making. By that time, matter has stopped spawning sporadically into our surroundings as we press deeper through the exterior-made burrow. We come upon a section of the tunnel with nine branching narrows, each a different size to the last.

The Answer doesn't miss a beat: "Come, this way," she says, as she leads me down the third narrow from the left of the section.

It's a winding passage, which takes us through portions of the narrow which see vortexes spewing from the ground. We have to watch our step so as not to step through any. Where they lead, I don't know. She whispers to herself as we bustle along.

"And that's five." The Answer speaks aloud, as she points at the last vortex we make it past.

"Now watch this." She says with a grin, as she turns right and pushes against the oceanic sky that forms the tunnel walls. Like a doorway hinged from its bottom, that piece of the tunnel swings open with a fall, turning the piece of sky she just pushed at into a walkway, which seems to extend as we walk across it. To every side of the walkway we are surrounded by emptiness. It's not as if we're in an unfilled room. It feels like if I step off of the walkway we're on, I might dissipate into some state of null. A scary concept even for me.

"You're lucky you came when you did," she says breaking the silence of our walking. "You get to see Else fill."

As she speaks, our surroundings, or lack thereof, take on a blank, colorless hue. Slowly, the blankness around us is filled by an array of patches, of varying consistencies. Some patches radiate shining luminescent light, others vibrating to unverified frequencies. Each patch carries with it a distinct texture and appearance, so soon the empty void is full of an assortment of distinct backgrounds pressed up beside each other in an overlapping patchwork. It's quite a beautiful display.

"They're fragments of existence caught drifting through elsewhere being integrated. This is how Else develops," she explains.

One by one, the patches indent against the environment producing outward spherical depth, before shooting off towards their own quadrants in every direction. I watch as each patch then stretches indefinitely into an all-encompassing background, layering atop the background patch before it. It's as if each patch-made horizon makes up its own sprawling world within Else as it covers the next. It must span undefinable length in totality. We continue to walk on the suspended walkway. Below, I can even see ground forming from some of the patches stretching all around us.

"Isn't it splendid?" She says, looking my way.

I can't deny the awe-inducing magnitude of it all.

"Yeah. I've never seen anything like this."

I try not to be too distracted by the switching exteriors out of reluctance to fall off the walkway and become enveloped by that world for another few decades. Nonetheless, I find it difficult to ignore the marvel of whole horizons coming into being.

The Answer stops and grabs my hand.

"Over here," she says, beaming my way. She jumps ahead, dragging us both into a fall through the walkway where I imagined we would've stepped. I brace myself for a hard impact but find that we land on a soft patch of turf. In front of us stands an odd house of unplaceable design. Not quite mansion-sized but by no means small. It looks stitched together. That's honestly the best way to put it.

"We're here!" The Answer exclaims.

"You seem to know your way quite well," I say.

"I've been here for a while now. It intrigues me. For everything so set in stone in *places*, Else is dynamic. You can never be too certain about what's going to happen."

"There hasn't been a dull moment so far, that's for certain," I add.

"Just wait until you see it go through its shifts."

I have no idea what she means by that, but if nothing I've seen before now constitutes Else going through "its shifts", then I know I'm in for quite the show for when it does.

"Are you coming?" She pulls her tongue at me, as she walks on ahead towards the front doorstep of the house. I follow steadily behind her.

"Welcome to my humble abode! Built it with my own two hands."

"Out of what?"

It didn't look like any conventional materials could've made up the walls to this home.

"Anything I could find once I got here. And anything that appeared. I had to get pretty good at architecture," she says as she opens the door and we step inside.

I want to ask her how she managed to get all the materials to stick, but I feel like I have more pressing items to attend to. I had come all this way for a reason.

Embodiments didn't need to eat, sleep or breathe, but could engage in such activities at their own leisure. As such, The Answer's home had no use for a kitchen or any sort of dining quarters. Despite this, she produces a hand-made mug filled with a shimmering green liquid after bringing me to her living room. We sit on boulder looking objects placed on either side of the quaint room. I would've thought our seats would be hard to the touch by the look of them, but I sink right into the object as I sit back into it.

"It's not poisonous, I assure you. I saw a critter drinking

from a pool of the stuff months ago, so I stocked up on as much of it as possible. It's really quite good!"

"Thanks," I say as I take a sip.

It must be something of an acquired taste. The liquid isn't harsh to the tongue, but it carries with it a certain pungent flavoring that is hard to describe. Not even the effect that resources in Else have on my senses is straightforward. Figures.

Within a few more sips, I'm still not having an easier time placing the flavor, but I am becoming more used to the overall experience of drinking it. It could grow on me with time. Then again, I need to do what I came here for, so that might not be a given.

"So what brought you to Else?" I start.

"Me? Boredom. I needed a bit of excitement in my life and Else just happened to be where I landed up."

"The journey, it must've tested you at every turn."

"Not really. You could say it just came to me."

"That's incomprehensible," I interject. "Else might as well be short for *elusive* for how improbable it is to *just* reach. For you to say that, there must be more to it than just your words. I think I've got you figured out. "

"Oh? And what do you mean by that?"

"I think you know. It's you, your expression. It must've helped you find your way."

"Interesting." The Answer can't hold back her smile. "And what would you decree my expression might be? Be careful now, I may judge you for your answer," she giggles.

I put the mug down as I stare The Answer in the eyes. Blonde streaks of hair conceal the intricacies of her face. Even so, they can't hide her stunning beauty, or the consuming gaze of her blue eyes. These were important moments: embodiments conversing about their expressions.

You couldn't hope to get more personal and now, finally, was the time for me to voice my hypothesis.

"You *know* things. About me even. Like Else being *where areas don't tend to be*, and you describing things the way I understand them to be," I say.

"And then you mention Attain– as if you knew me getting here involved her," I add.

"Only someone who'd been with me could know those things, but we've never met before now. I didn't have to tell you anything before you already knew it. That's your expression, isn't it? You've got *explanations* for everything, don't you?"

The Answer sits quietly for a moment. I had interpreted her as an embodiment and I felt confident that I was correct. The Answer could explain things, and as for the questions I asked— how she knew to so eloquently put them in a way tailored to my understanding. I keep my eyes fixed on hers. Pride swells in my chest as I see her prepare to reply, no doubt in confirmation of my hypothesis.

I see a frown emerge on her face.

Did I say something wrong?

Did my guess hurt her?

"You... were close."

My chest sinks.

How could I have been wrong? Everything I had said to her made sense. I-

"I'm *Answer*, not *Explain*, if there is one. Hmm." She pauses for a second to put her index finger and thumb to her chin "There isn't. At least not yet."

How does she know that?

"I contain the answers, it's that simple. For those questions that you asked me, the answers were expressible through explanations, yes, but answers themselves can take on many other forms than that."

Oh. That must've been how she gave me those explanations which so closely aligned with my understanding of Else. She had given me the most suitable answer to account for what I had already gathered.

"Then when you asked me how I knew you'd be here, you'd had the answer all along?"

"In a sense, it was always there."

"Then why ask?"

"Because in asking the question, an answer became available for me to know."

Then why not just ask the question to herself and become privy to the answer? She had given me the chance to reply.

"Plus, I wanted to hear what you would have to say," the embodiment adds.

So when she wasn't satisfied with the answer I gave her, she must've accessed the answer that matched what she wanted to know.

"Getting to Else then, that must've been because you knew the answer to its whereabouts?"

"Still no. When I said it came to me, I meant that. I can interact with answers too, you know. I needed to find something that could alleviate my boredom. So Else presented itself as an answer, literally. After that, it was as simple as stepping through a doorway to the destination," she grinned.

By the sounds of it, her expression was quite invaluable.

"You could say I *manage the result*. That's what answers are, the result which fulfills any given prompt. It's only a matter of what the prompt is for me to inherit the result which fulfills it: the answer," the namesake explains.

That was even more impressive than I had conceived. I was sorely off-the-mark when I assumed what Answer could express was solely explanations. For simply needing a result which could bring her excitement, her prompt, Answer had called Else towards herself to fulfill her desire (an answer), a destination which took me decades to reach by comparison.

"Any prompt... that's a pretty expansive range," I say, as a sense of excitement begins to well up inside of me. I came here to find the answer. And here Answer was, more than I could have ever imagined.

"Yes, yes. When I first *emerged,* drawing the answers from any prompts which caught my interest was quite the pastime."

"I imagine you must have learned a good many things."

"I did. Until eventually I felt myself ready to begin answering prompts."

"That makes it sound like you chose the answers yourself," I say.

"You heard correctly, then. Perhaps you'd like to know what makes it all so special?"

"It all? As in, ALL of it?" I look around for a moment before turning back to her. She was describing entirety here.

"Precisely. At least it all up to this point."

"Enlighten me."

"In a word: Irregularity."

She really just gave me an answer about everything that feels like it fits. Not to mention, there's something about that answer coming out of her mouth that makes it feel... legitimized. I just know I can trust what she says. I finally think I'm beginning to understand Answer based on everything she's told me.

Every equation poses some kind of query. If Else could be described as the unincluded variable to one, then Answer was the bearer of whatever the result of the equation may be, that is, if I was understanding her correctly. She could reveal what all the working out of the equation led up to. And what's more, she was Answer herself, so I assumed she must've been the conclusion to some given equation, maybe multiple, perhaps the culmination of the cosmos itself's very own quest for a result that could answer every other query, embodied. And there that answer was, sitting across from me.

"Irregularity... That does have a ring to it. I like that."

"I'm happy you think so. It took me a while to consider it enough to be sure. Personally, It's one of my favorite answers."

"About that. It's about time I told you why I came all the way."

"Go ahead."

"I came to Else with the knowledge that a certain something resided within it. The Answer. I now know that to be you. I've found you here to request..."

"You want an answer, don't you?"

"But you said you wouldn't..."

"I don't have to. I've heard more versions of this conversation than you could care to know," she says, frowning again, as if I had done something of personal insult to her.

"Let me guess, you want to know life's meaning?"

That one couldn't hurt to know, but-

"No. I didn't come here with any questions for you. I came to learn."

"Hmm. That's different. And you thought I might make a good teacher?" She asks.

"I thought if anything could instill me with elevational insight, it'd be the answer. And to discover you are an embodiment, like me, only makes the prospect all the more enticing."

"Okay, I like the way you put that. As if being here with me is some kind of once in a lifetime meeting," she smiles wide, indicating that any previous judgments had been eradicated, if only for a moment.

"It might as well be. I may not look it, but I awakened a staggering number of years ago," I say, though I preferred not to say when I emerged.

"Since then," I continue, "I have seen magnificent, terrible things. Explored extensively. And been present through many speech-defying occasions. But now more than ever, I realize that if I'm to keep going, it'll only happen given an opportunity to educate myself through learning from someone like you."

"I feel honored that you think so. I could enjoy helping you out," she says.

"Thank you." I say, with genuine appreciation.

"First lesson. I won't give answers easily. You need to earn them."

"I find that acceptable. What are your terms?"

"You'll have to do something for me if you want to hear what I've got to say."

"Anything."

"You need to give me... an answer of your own. And a good one at that."

"I thought you already had all the answers."

"Yes, I contain them. But I don't always have to look. I'll try not to take a peek at your answer. Besides, it'll make it more fun that way," She flashes her now unmistakably playful grin.

Okay. She's smiling again. Don't fuck this up.

"A lot of things seem to be about fun to you. What about Else particularly made it so exciting?" I ask, stalling for time. It's a good thing she wasn't looking within herself for my answer. If she did she would only find herself coming up short. I haven't yet thought of an enriching answer to tell her.

"Being anywhere with defined traits, a place, I found the answers started to come too easy. How hard do you think it was for me to glean answers about the world I was living in, when everything was as face value as up being up, down staying down, and sides remaining lateral? It came to the point where I started being able to guess the answers about places before I needed anything to prompt them. The fluidity of Else presented me with unpredictability that's made pinning down its nature to answers at all somewhat of an exercise I've grown fond of. I enjoy the fact that on any given day here, an answer I already have about it may change with the flux of the surroundings. It keeps things fresh."

So, she liked the novelty that Else could bring her. Constantly seeking novelty– it was one of the same weaknesses I had picked up over my unending lifespan. It reminds me of myself. Too much.

I feel the pang of my right hand. It's a familiar throb that I can't help but feel may serve as my answer. I can't remember what it's supposed to mean, but I know it's been the answer I needed before- No. I can't rely on that. Not here. Something about it doesn't feel right. I'm not about to drag Answer down the path I took that led me to whatever these aches are beckoning.

My thoughts take me to an alternative: I recall meeting a certain interloper in the space between somewhere and nowhere, that I now know to be elsewhere, thanks to Answer. The interloper named *Ratio*, who supposed he could reveal a way for me to get to Else. We had met before, nearly a century prior, although the circumstances were not as amicable as this time around. The last time we saw each other was violent– we were both young, carrying inflamed passions which led to more than one encounter where instead of treating each other like fellow embodiments, we acted as sworn combatants.

Thankfully that time was over now though, and the next

time I saw Ratio his presence only served to improve my situation.

I'd spent what must've been months soaring through the metallic-silver vista of Elsewhere, unable to stumble upon Else when mid-flight, I found myself coming face to face with Ratio. He was sitting crossed-legged with his arms to either side in meditation on a large piece of debris drifting through the region. I didn't recognize him at first, but he was the first entity I'd seen with opposable thumbs since I made it out of mappable parts; I had to stop to make contact with this stranger in my view. Long locks of hair concealed his face, but I could make out the markings of what looked to be a golden spiral on his right arm. That alone should have given me a clue.

"Hello fellow!" I announced as I sat down in front of him.

The stranger didn't so much as move from the serene, meditative pose he was in.

"Greetings. Perhaps you didn't hear me there?" I repeated, closer now.

"Can't you tell. I'm busy," the concealed stranger replied.

"I see that. My apologies, but I have a question to ask of you."

"... That voice. Brings me back." The stranger stood up and pulled back his hair.

"... You!" It took me a moment to recognize his face. It had matured. I instinctively readied myself into a combative stance as I jumped a step back.

"Endless. It's been a while." He continued calmly.

"Ratio. What are you doing here?" I couldn't hide my disdain. All I could remember as I gazed upon his face, was the relentless way in which he had attacked me all those years ago.

"Relax. I'm not going to fight you."

"Forgive me if your words don't put me to ease," I said back.

"I've changed since then." He took a casual step forward and his gaze sharpened. "You on the other hand, don't look like you've aged a decade."

Courtesy of my expression, I mused silently.

"Well, I can assure you I've been through my fair share since then too, though that's besides the point. Why are you here?" I still hadn't lowered my stance, call it a precautionary measure.

"I'm allowed to be anywhere, aren't I? There isn't any rule saying I can't be here, now is there?"

"I suppose you're right..."

"Then settle down Endless, I'm not your enemy, nor do I want to be anymore. Let's put the past to rest."

"Fine, I'll take your word for it," I said as I lowered my stance.

"Good. That phrase reminds me of a story I once heard that changed the way I look at things. Perhaps you'd like to hear it?" He asked.

"I'm currently on a search. For a destination I heard can only be reached between Somewhere and Nowhere."

"Ah. So that's why you're so far removed from anywhere an atlas could bring you. I know of where you speak. Else. That's a tricky one to get to."

"Are you familiar with these parts?"

"You could say I've been around. This region makes for particularly good practice."

"In what sense?" I decided to entertain him in hopes that it might lead to me acquiring information about finding Else.

"Nothing here is static, this region and everything in it are in a continuous state of re-arrangement. It would be hard to try and describe it as an area with the way it refuses to conform to any outline. That makes things tough for me as I try to scan its totality."

Scan. That's right. Ratio could do that.

"How good have you gotten?"

"Enough that I can keep up with moving targets," Ratio replies.

"Look to your right in three seconds. You'll find three surprises."

I turn at the preordained moment. First, a massive blue comet soars through my field of vision. Off it, breaks a piece of debris. Debris that upon closer inspection looks like a bath-tub. And finally, when Ratio says "Now look up," I make out a four-point star that bursts into Elsewhere locality with a twinkle.

I grin.

"Then you could get a read on Else's whereabouts?"

"It isn't beyond my wildest capabilities."

"Will you help me find it?"

"If only to prove to you I'm different from back then. I can give you scans of the most erratic sectors darting through this region. Else might just be one of them. The ratios I deduce from the scans may bring you important insight into the proportion of Else to the rest of the region. You might find there's a mathematical pattern to where the destination shows up next."

"Alright. Give it a shot."

"Okay." Ratio clasped his hands together before stretching them out to either side of himself. Suddenly, every fiber of my being felt as though it were being put under a lens. I shivered. It hadn't been long enough since I had experienced that feeling.

"You're trying to analyze me, aren't you?" I asked.

"I deduce now. And you still take that far too personally."

Back when I encountered Ratio, he attempted to use his

expression on me. He could examine any subject and find the ratios which existed within them. Those ratios could tell him many things: the structure of the subject, their capacity, and even the fault lines that existed within them. He tried to analyze all three in me back then, in the hopes that he could defeat me in combat and prove his superiority as an embodiment. It hadn't gone as well as he had intended.

"You're a part of the radius I'm extending through this region, so it goes without saying that your ratios are getting approximated too. Besides, I'm still getting nothing from you. You're lucky, Endless. I'll have you calculated, eventually."

"You won't get anywhere dedicating your time trying to explain me," I said.

"You call it dedication. I just call it doing what I emerged for."

I had never considered it in that way. Though he'd have a difficult time if he ever wanted to find a ratio to me. The best I could imagine was 1:1. One everlasting embodiment, me, to the one word which could encapsulate everything that described me...

"I'm endless down to my very essence, how could you ever hope to express that through ratio?"

Ratio smirked and pointed at the spiral marking on his arm: "You see this? It's the Golden Ratio. And it extends irrationally to no completion. It just *keeps going*. For as long as it extends, so does my longevity. "

"I'm... impressed" Usually, embodiments tended to last as long as *their namesake* availed them the opportunity to last. For me, it was as simple as being endless– there wasn't much more to it. For other embodiments though, they had to find their ways to prolong their lives, if they wanted that much. Living to no end had numerous benefits, not least of all being able to explore without fear of there ever being a lack of time, but outliving any companions who might join me on those expeditions proved a harsh reminder that not all life around me could so defiantly press on.

Whenever I met someone who found a way to cheat or work their way around age limits, it brought me a particularly deep joy, knowing there would be another individual who I might cross paths with again down the ever-lengthening line. I felt the same way about Ratio, even if we did have our differences once before.

"We both know that isn't me, though," I say.

I understood enough about basic maths to understand that by assuming the same structure as the Golden Ratio's length, Ratio had effectively extended his life near incalculably, but if he thought that meant he had me figured out, he would still have a long way to go before he ever started to understand me. The key difference between my longevity and his was that I had no end, period; while Ratio's longevity, riding the length of the Golden Ratio, had no *foreseeable* end due to the extending nature of the irrational number.

"True. But for every decimal place the number expands, I get another moment of life to live. Stars will stop pulsating before there's a complete approximation of pi or phi. That means I've still got a long time coming to deduce yours and many other ratios. Rest assured though, deducing your ratio is not one of my highest priorities anymore," Ratio said.

"Good. Maybe at some point you'll find enough interesting subjects that I'll fall off of your radar completely. How is your scan of this... region coming along?" It was hard to call it anything but a region. It shifted far too often to be called a place or a defined location. And as Ratio said, it didn't even follow enough of an outline to be deemed an area.

"It takes time. It's pretty difficult scanning a target that doesn't even move linearly. At this point I still have to find it."

From what I was gathering, it was difficult to describe Else as 'there'. To be 'there', or more specifically, 'over there', the subject had to be stagnant enough to describe in terms of positioning. Areas could fit that description. They were the points on a map, so long as you could find one that zoomed out enough to capture them, or had enough layers to account for them, even when moving. Take the area of a piece of land on a stray planet. Or even the planet itself. While the planet is in motion as it rotates and orbits around the largest mass in its stellar vicinity, it could still be pinned down on an astronomical map.

This same principle applies to planes of existence. For any place and location, there are always ways to represent them cartographically if you use the right measure. Those areas could be 'there'. Else however, spent its days off any kind of map. For any tool to measure or pinpoint where *there* was, Else inherently existed outside of it, as Else existed wherever the radar wasn't looking. That, understandably, made Ratio's attempts to scan for Else an uphill battle. He was an embodiment though, and not a map, so I had the slightest bit of hope that he would prevail in his sweep of the region.

"You might as well take a seat, this may take a while," Ratio continued.

I wasn't pressed for time, but I didn't necessarily want to take the sidetrack of having to sit around and wait.

"I can tell you don't like the sound of that. Remember, this is my favor to you. But I'll do you one more. I can keep you entertained. How about you listen to that story I told you about. The one that changed me. It's one I think every embodiment should hear."

I weighed my options for a moment. Continuing to soar

aimlessly through where I would come to know as Elsewhere looking for Else, or take the opportunity to hear Ratio
out, in the case that his scan yielded some kind of naviga-
tional tip for finding my destination.

I took a seat. " Go on."

"Excellent. You won't be disappointed." Ratio said back,
hands still to his side. He then retrieved a notebook from the
ground.

While I did get to hear the story he had to tell, he never
did find Else in his scan, the destination living up to its
infamy for being so unfathomably out of reach. Yet this
story, I now realize, might make an excellent answer for a
certain embodiment sitting in front of me...

I turn to face Answer.

"It's a long answer but one all the same. Are you
prepared to accept that?"

"You're my first guest in ages! And an interesting one at
that. Of course I'll hear you out." She replies excitedly. "Just
go ahead and start when you're ready."

"I was hoping you'd say that," I say.

And so the story begins.

2 / LEXICON

LEXICON WAS one of the first embodiments to emerge. He was conceived once the combined meaning of all created words met the threshold necessary to become something more. A breathing continuance of words, from their previous state of non-living. More than that, Lexicon held a unique relationship with words themselves. They were his adjacents and he governed them well.

Lexicon embodied living language and as he who presided over words, his expression gave him the capacity to manipulate them in ways independent of writing or speech. Lexicon could, at his leisure, wield words and express whatever term he wished to use, resulting in a physical reaction. Upon his initial emergence, Lexicon found himself engulfed within a whirlwind. All around him a host of letters swirled. His very birthplace occurred between the syllables and consonants of every known and undiscovered dialect. It was a conceptual realm of words and as the living offspring of linguistics itself, Lexicon was quick to adapt to the domain of letters all around him. Reaching out his hand, Lexicon summoned letters from the alphabetical hurricane which surrounded him, until he had enough letters to build his very first word. Floating in his opened palm hovered one word: Ten.

Lexicon couldn't yet speak, but he had been born with a prescient knowledge of what words meant being the embodiment of colloquy itself. Lexicon didn't know how or why, but he knew that *ten* told him he was the tenth of his new and strange kind to emerge. Lexicon let the floating number disperse from his hand as he returned to the alphabetical whirlwind before him, calling a different set of letters from their flurry towards his outstretched hand. The suspended letters configured themselves into the word *embodiment,* telling Lexicon everything he needed to know about the kind of existence he was; he was the embodiment of a very specific concept.

Long after settling on a name for himself, there came a day where Lexicon felt ready to participate in the world who created his purpose. When he did, he pulled all of the letters surrounding him towards himself, allowing them to assimilate within him. Letter by letter, every syllable and consonant became a part of Lexicon, as the alphabetical whirlwind slowly permeated into his *geist*, leaving Lexicon standing in a new environment devoid of swirling script.

The embodiment of lexis spent his first days getting acclimated to the surroundings he found himself in. Unfamiliar sights filled his every gaze no matter where he looked. The Sun. The Sun.

Lexicon wasn't alone on this world, quickly, he found a bipedal race of existences atop this natural order.

Being a conceptual entity, Lexicon didn't have a form which this race of existences could see or interact with. To put it into understandable terms, let us equate the plane of existence this race lives in as the number 6. To this 6, any planes of existence below it such as 5 leading all the way down to 1, are perceivable and can be interacted with because those numbers can all fit within the scope of 6. Embodiments are conceptual beings, and thus first emerge on the conceptual plane of existence. For the sake of this analogy, the conceptual plane could be equated with a 7, thus putting it above the level of perception and intractability of 6.

Here, Lexicon roamed the world much like an apparition, intangible and undetectable to any and all life which inhabited it.

It didn't take long before he learnt how to manifest a form that was perceivable and intractable to those on planes of existence lower than the conceptual. By the time he could, he didn't even want to. But long before even that point this race of existences and him still shared a single unifier between them: namely, words.

This race of existences used words. They were the original creators of words, and in a way stemmed Lexicon's own birth from their languages. Being the embodiment of such mechanics, Lexicon held insight regarding any words he encountered, as he was quick to pick up on the fact that the bipeds used words to communicate, to convey emotional and philosophical expressions, to record history.

In turn, he was quick to identify the meaning behind what words they used. Lexicon learned that the race had a fondness for finding new ways to describe themselves in words. *Homo-sapiens* and *humans* were the words that stuck. Humans couldn't see Lexicon, but the fact that they used words was all the connection Lexicon needed in order to feel that he could grow to enjoy life on this world. It didn't take long before Lexicon had a grasp of all of the words humans used, such as carriages, buildings, or even the exquisite way they chose to define the fauna and flora who added beauty to their world.

As Lexicon spent more time amongst them, his responsibility as the embodiment of words became more clear to him. Lexicon was the inventor of new words, which meant that he was chief architect of that process. Humans never knew they had called upon Lexicon when they thought they were developing new words, and Lexicon spent his time experimenting with the fundamentals and structure of language; producing new combinations of script to create more holistic expressions of message.

What Lexicon found most interesting was new common meanings and variations of grammar humanity gave to the words he manufactured. When he watched humans come up with their own words, Lexicon would throw a few new letters and sound combinations their way. Whole languages were born due to Lexicon's involvement in creating words and letters for humanity to use. If a human stumbled upon a word he created and used it well enough to gain their fellow man or woman's popular approval, it would enter into regular use. That was the real test: whether man or an embodiment-made word would stick. It tended to lean human. Still, Lexicon spent a major fraction of his time toiling to the fashioning of new words for the usage of any beings who made use of language for their communication, even outside of its original architects.

Words that didn't garner widespread approval would be relegated to gibberish and cast aside. Lexicon didn't mind forgetting those, after all, he saw that humans existed in a realm based on trial and error. And by the late 20th century, Lexicon had amassed a vast collective of words which he crafted for humanity and any other species to use, leaving some words for only his own usage. Lexicon could've traveled to meet any of those races other than humanity that used his words, by simply wielding the word *appear* to cause the physical reaction of *appearing* at his desired location, but Lexicon had taken a liking to this so-called 'Earth,' ever since he'd encountered it after exiting the lettered whirlwind he had absorbed.

There were eras on Earth's timeline which left Lexicon disappointed in its inhabitants, however. During times of great global strife, dictatorial regimes would emerge all around the world. Throughout such periods, the authoritarian regimes would implement strategies to control their populaces. One such method for control was in constricting the word usage of the given populace, to words that suited the regime's agenda, and leaders manipulated this power by changing the meaning of words and integrating phrases that would sway the populace towards a certain stance.

Lexicon bore witness to these machinations across time in which authoritarian regimes would seek to control language, and it disturbed him to no end. Lexicon was an embodiment, and as such felt himself separate from any world of politics the humans entertained in their hierarchical or laissez-faire societal structures. Lexicon's responsibility was to ensure that there was always a lexis from which humanity could collect new words to use.

It was wounding to discover whole organizations of society, those of whom blessed with the freedom of diction, were now controlling words and using them as weapons. He never intended for speech to be anything less than a free horizon for communicators to discover and explore the wealth of words that Lexicon had created for them. It soon became clear to Lexicon that even the original creators of words, humans could not be trusted to hold the responsibility of handling words without attempts to manipulate the way those words were used. They were more error than trial.

Even worse were the many inflammatory ways humans found to break each other even outside of organized politics. Words that made Lexicon shudder. Words like *nigger,* which reduced those of black ancestry to beings unworthy of equality. Or *untermensch*, another word developed to categorize fellow humans of jewish ancestry as a 'lower breed'. Slut was just as evil, a word Lexicon learned was used to degrade any woman who did not conform to the oppressive standards set by mortal men– and man, held great power over all else.

Those kind of words never stopped coming. That was when Lexicon decided that if he could not guide humanity to elevate their language then he would take words away and see how well they fared then. Despite their abominations, he wanted to see whether or not they could come up with something they wouldn't try to exercise unneeded control or hatred over.

"I'll take your word for it," was the first sentence humans heard Lexicon utter, and he chose that phrase cognizant of corrupting its original meaning. While it was true that they couldn't see or interact with Lexicon in his conceptual state, wielding the word *listen*, Lexicon made himself loud and clear to his desired targets. Confused as to where the voice was coming from, most humans brushed it off as if they were simply hearing a sound that wasn't there. For the humans that did inquire about where the voice came from, no answers could be drawn... Nonetheless Lexicon had spoken, and he meant what he had said. Lexicon was taking their words literally, and there would be nothing humanity or any other race could do about it.

At his own discretion, Lexicon began to remove word after word from the lexicons of humanity and any races which made use of words for their language. He had decided that only he, the embodiment of words, was worthy enough to use them. It didn't take long for humanity to begin to become a mumbling husk of their former articulate selves. Whole books were reduced to sets of blank pages, making it impossible to ignore the fact that something had gone very wrong for humanity in losing their words. With what little terms of expression they had left, humanity attempted to find out why they were suddenly losing their ability to speak to each other as even those who used sign language found that words were becoming unintelligible to them.

The last straw came when Lexicon took the word *free*– a day which marked a dark turn for Lexicon's own moral compass. Suddenly, he had taken the one word from humanity which should have defined them as a unified civilization... The United States of America, the land of the — meek. This created hysteria among people who didn't even have the words to express their terror anymore. Without words, society found itself crumbling, and in humanity's distress, they called out to whoever could help them however they could.

THOUGHT WAS a gathering of mental conception accumulated into an embodiment. An entity comprised of psyche, Thought resided in the mental realm– the realm of psyche– born of the collective consciousness of life. There, thoughts traveled like signals, while telepathic projections roamed the plane like wild beasts. Resting atop this psychological landscape stood Thought; the apex of the mental food-chain. Thought spent most of their days maintaining order among the occupants of the mental realm, keeping ideas from crossing one another and ensuring telepathic projections did not wreak havoc upon the plane. Very little in the way of mishaps occurred with Thought at the helm of the mental realm. They served as its venerable defender.

There were points however, where Thought would have to leave the mental realm to perform duties in the physical realm. Assignments such as guarding an important thought which was destined to arrive to the mind of some lifeform, or lending aid through the combat of rogue thoughts in risk of becoming corporal. This was often the case with power-hungry and strong-minded civilizations.

On this particular occasion, Thought was called towards

the physical realm through the individual cries of a world still in its earliest of infancies in terms of its inhabitants' ability to astrally extend their minds. There was something strange in the telepathic gift Thought had in receiving their messages. It was clear just how puerile this race was when it came to their own telepathic abilities, as they still relied on physical language to send and receive messages rather than metaphysical transmittance.

Even more strange was that it appeared as though the inhabitants of this world could not string together a coherent sentence, even given the disadvantage with their vernacular communication. As if they were at a loss for words and due to this, Thought could easily recognize that the race was in trouble. With so many telepathic voices crying out simultaneously, Thought took it upon themself to handle the problem.

What Thought finds in the physical realm is a sight they have never seen before. Pandemonium grips the population of Earth, as its inhabitants scramble without means of communication. Their *general will* had unknowingly called out to Thought through pure distress. They had no way of communicating conventionally besides grunts and mumbles, as suddenly, humanity found itself stretched far past the limits of civility. Thought knew that for a race so inexperienced in the ways of mental communication, it was concerning that their despair was so strong it had penetrated the extents of the mental realm. In other words, it was wrong that humanity was suddenly capable of sending out mental-eruptions at all. It was far beyond their evolutionary aptitude at that point. The result could only mean grave damage to their minds the longer these signals uncontrollably emanated from their psyches.

Thought could tell extreme distress had forced them into the corner where a latent psychic potential had emerged from, but they weren't sure why. Deciding it was better they stay non-corporal, Thought journeys around Earth at the speed of thought, searching for a solution. Thought focuses on avoiding human thought-waves for the risk that if one of the thought-waves hit them, it might send a psychic reeling back to whichever human the mental-emanation came from. If this occurred it would expose Thought's existence and position to the unready mind.

Eventually, Thought came across one, clear telepathic sentence most Earthlings seemed to be able to convey: *I'll take your word for it.* Unable to comprehend the significance of that particular sentence, it lends one small clue as to where the struggle of articulation has stemmed from. From the sheer magnitude of humans telepathically projecting that one string of words, Thought realizes it must've come from an unknown source. They scan the minds of humans everywhere, in a sweep to try and discover where the sentence has originated from. No logical explanation found- only a fragmented memory of some brief voice...

Take your word for it...

Investigating further, Thought finds that no records of words exist on the planet. While Thought wasn't necessarily a speaker of any of Earth's languages, they can still decode the message received through telepathic data. This was how Thought could understand what the humans meant, despite their lack of connection to Earth. What Thought finds across text is that words are disappearing from the pages they were written in, and that humanity has lost a critical amount of word usage. What's interesting is that the sequence in which specific words have been disappearing seems random. But for all of the words disappearing, there are a handful that remain amongst the words being lost.

From the words that stay, Thought quickly deciphers a message that has been intentionally left behind for the inhabitants of Earth, as if some words were pried from their very mouths, while others were imbedded as some sort of lesson.

It is at that point that Thought understands that whatever is going on is far more sinister than humanity stumbling into mental advancements above their capacity. Some external force is forcing the words away from them. Once Thought is convinced of this fact, they quickly alter their search parameters. Instead of searching for human thought patterns to find out what is going on, they set their sights on any other existences which might be active on Earth. After sifting through the vast array of fauna, some of which having higher telepathic potential than humans, such as the hive-minded colonies of insects, and flora, which indeed gave off the slightest hints of psychic emanations, Thought finds their mark as their inquisition lends a presence distinct from any earthly biology. In fact, Thought recognizes the mental signature as somewhat familiar. Like one of their own. An embodiment.

⸻

Sometime and place in the far flung future...
Within a suspended translucent case, against the backdrop of an Andromeda galaxy, spatial points of fracture cracked in space just outside of their box.

"Are you sure about this?" The woman asked.

The man checked his watch.

"I couldn't be more so."

"Meddling with history though... It's dangerous."

"I wouldn't call what I do meddling, more correcting. Besides, there isn't anyone more qualified to alter the course of things than me." The man admits.

"You say that, but it's always me who ends up being hands on in your execution." The woman posits.

"You're the only one I can trust to do this given your skillset, when instances such as these arise. "

"I know. But that doesn't make changing the sequence of events feel any less significant."

"Getting cold feet now, after all our work? To your point, I don't disagree. However, in this case, the entire timeline is in danger of collapse. It is crumbling at its foundations due to the actions of a rogue. The only reason we're still able to speak right now is because you've halted the effects of that embodiment from reaching us." The man says.

"For now. I can't hold this back forever. There are just too many words to stop from being taken." *Prevention* says, as she holds together the box which serves to prevent words from being taken from their very own conversation.

"That's why we need to act now. The unconstricted progress of this world relies on it. We have already lost one pivotal facet of existence we can't even verbalize any longer. How many more must we lose before something is done? "

"If I fail, how can you be sure we won't end up with a worse outcome?"

"You haven't before, and you won't now. You have the intel, and your mission. Now, are you ready to go? I can send you back to around where this all started," *Time* replies.

"I'm only doing this because the alternative is oblivion. Not even we can live like that. Do it."

Time stretches his hand towards Prevention : "Very well. When we meet again, let it be with *liberty*."

Out of Time's hand pours a stream of *the past* which envelops Prevention like a cloud. The cloud of past begins bonding with Prevention, as it circles around and enters her. When Prevention's skin makes contact with the cloud, she immerses into it altogether. Before long, Prevention has nearly completely dispersed into the cloud. With only her neck up remaining, Prevention has just enough time to get in her last words to Time: "I hope you remember me."

Watching his companion fade from sight, Time clenches his outstretched hand as the cloud condenses into a swirling tornado of minuscule proportions. In an ouroboros, the tornado consumes itself until it disappears from existence altogether, or more specifically, from *their present.*

"I always remember." Time says as he finds himself standing alone. "Mission success, I'll be seeing you," Time says, as he looks at his dispersing hand.

In the background of space, the cracks splinter into lattice, and a bolt-like shard is ejected into the deep of space.

For a second Thought freezes. Then presses towards this new presence. Thought finds the embodiment's mental signature on an island off the coast of Africa. The signature resides in a vacated home in Stone Town– Zanzibar, Tanzania, specifically. With a courteous knock on the door, Thought waits for a few moments before deciding to skip formalities, and steps into the house where the perceived presence of an embodiment lingers.

"And who might you be?" A voice comes from one of the rooms inside of the home.

"I go by Thought."

"Woah... That's not coming from your voice..."

"My apologies. I naturally communicate like this."

"I think I'm getting a headache."

"Verbal communication is acceptable," Thought says.

"Okay. Cool. What are you doing here, Thought?"

"I know you're the only other one like me on this planet.

I'm looking for a reason as to why words are being taken from this world," they say.

"And... what do you plan on doing once you've gotten your answer?" the voice questions.

"Help in any way I can."

"You would help the humans?" the voice asks.

"You could say they've stumbled their way into my territory. They shouldn't be there. I merely wish to resolve that issue," Thought says.

"And that would take what exactly?"

"Returning their words to them."

"Then we find ourselves aligned." The voice steps into the clear view of Thought. A 5'7 woman of unmatched composure. Her spiky hair bountifully fixed to the point of most sharpness.

"I am Prevention. I was sent to this planet to try and combat the taking of words," the embodiment says.

"Then why are these people still unable to use them?"

"By the time I arrived here, it was too late. The taking of words had already begun. And the culprit is nowhere to be found."

"Culprit? What do you mean?"

"This isn't just happening because of nature. There is an embodiment like us, causing this," Prevention explains.

"Who?" Thought asks.

"He goes by Lexicon, and according to what I've been told, he is the embodiment of words."

"The embodiment of words... He'd exercise his expression in such a way?"

"It appears so. But it's more than that. Where I come from, the effects of Lexicon taking words exact a far greater toll. A toll that might even involve the likes of you."

"Tell me. Everything," Thought says.

"Lexicon's seizing of words doesn't end with humanity. It

spreads. It spreads all the way until every living being is restricted from making use of them. Soon, it even affects the livelihoods of embodiments," Prevention continues.

A bead of concentrated concern runs down Thought's now physical body upon hearing this.

"In what way?" They question.

"Embodiments are emergences that fully personify a certain concept. You are Thought, and so must be the personification of the concept of the psyche?"

"I know that much about our race," they say.

"Yes, but it is more than that. I am Prevention. In other words, you could say I stop things. A stop could just as well be a pause. Preventing something from moving could be described as such, no? One might take those facts and incorrectly assume that I should therefore be Pause or Stop. To resolve the discrepancy of my identity before I emerged, a tether was needed to ground me in the concept I personify," Prevention pauses meaningfully to ensure her receiver is following along.

"That tether was the word Prevention," she continues. "It fully encapsulated what I am the embodiment of, while pausing and stopping are simply attributes of the act of prevention. That slight nuance is one which could only be elaborated through the use of a medium such as words. And as such, I only emerged after a clear enough link between what I personified, and the concept that could describe me was formed."

"The word gave you definition..." Thought trails off.

"Yes. And for many embodiments that may be the case. A word might be needed to ground them enough in existence for them to emerge. But with Lexicon taking words, that means that those embodiments may lack the tether they need to emerge."

"I see the issue. However, you said the toll of this might

even reach me. I emerged long before words did. How might this affect me?" Thought inquires.

"We do not live in a vacuum, Thought. What affects the birth of innumerable embodiments will come to affect you. Embodiments play a role in the continuance of existence. We emerge at necessary points when a concept necessitates a living manifestation to progress it. Creating a whole new entity that exudes that concept, it becomes the responsibility of that embodiment to maintain their concept's prominence in existence. In other words, while we still have them- because each embodiment acts as a pillar for existence, holding up the specific concept which they personify; just knowing you are an embodiment, I could assume you probably hold some kind of authority when it comes to the concept you epitomize."

Prevention is entirely correct. Thought's responsibility as the embodiment of mental conception was to maintain order within the mental realm, the realm of the psyche. Thought had never questioned why they acted as the chief protector of all things mental. But Prevention's explanation answered why Thought had always felt an intrinsic sense of duty to manage the mental intricacies of existence.

"You're saying we have purposes?"

"We have inclinations. Each wholly independent of what any other embodiments may be. Each as different to the next embodiment as the concept they personify. We do have the choice not to fulfill any inclinations we so feel, but being the personification of certain concepts, I have found that many embodiments do end up finding their own ways to act which advance the continuance of their specific concept. In so doing, progressing existence itself as the concepts unfold. I myself am existence's mechanism to prevent certain outcomes from being reached, which is why I am here." Prevention finishes.

"I think I understand. You want to stop Lexicon from taking words to maintain the natural flow of embodiments emerging," they say.

"Correct. If Lexicon continues to take words away, countless embodiments will lose the tethers they need to emerge. And without those embodiments to hold up the concepts they're meant to epitomize, existence will find itself buckling with no embodiments to keep it progressing."

"This Lexicon... He has to be stopped. Where did you learn of this embodiment?"

Prevention had no intention of telling Thought the era she had been sent from: "That isn't for you to know."

"Fine. Lexicon must be stopped all the same."

"So we agree. What do you intend to do?" Prevention asks.

"Find him, and get him to give words back, starting with humanity."

"I've been on Earth for little over a week now, and I've been unable to locate Lexicon," Prevention admits.

"I couldn't find any other mental signatures like ours either..." Thought says.

"Then he's in the wind."

"Wait. Maybe if I extend my search..." Thought says.

Reaching deep through their expression, Thought makes a mental scan intended to span as wide as the closest galactic superclusters. It would take too long for a mental-sonar wave to cross that distance at the speed of thought, so Thought opts to receive any direct mental-pings of life, from any life forms within their search field. Working through the perception of a grand tapestry of consciousness across Space.

Thought stands in place for what feels like minutes as Prevention silently watches and waits, before their eyes flash open and they begin to speak.

"I can feel it– the same kind of mental-cries that humanity have been emanating. Gah! Spreading like wildfire across the universe. I can't tell the start point of the cries. They're too unintelligible. Lexicon could be anywhere among them."

"Then it's already begun. Lexicon has started taking words from more than just humanity... It won't be long until he takes words away from his own kind."

"I won't let that happen. There are now too many telepathically-active beings who aren't ready for that stage. That mental-fallout produced through their emanations threatens to destabilize the mental-realm. That could wreak havoc on the corporal world," Thought says.

"So what will you do?" Prevention asks

"... I have an idea."

"If I can't track Lexicon, then I'll just have to find someone who can stop these words from being taken."

"And who might that be?"

"You must've heard of her. One of the first to emerge. They call her the chronicler. "

"You think you can find her?"

"I know I can. I'm going to find *Dictionary*. What will you do, Prevention?"

"I've given you the intel I know. Hopefully it serves you well in finding and stopping Lexicon. I trust that it will. I've got another mission and that's to retrieve a word Lexicon has held hostage. That word is tethered to an embodiment the world needs."

"What is the word?" Thought asks.

"Freedom. There will come a time when not even embodiments can say it. And that will be when it is already too late to save him."

"Let both of our tasks be favored by good fortune then."

"Indeed," Prevention nods.

And with that, Thought and Prevention part ways, both determined to achieve their goals.

Thought scours far and wide, until finally, they find their destination three weeks later. It had taken them that long to search for any thoughts which could point them in the direction of the embodiment they intended to find. Once they had found a lead, they set course for it.

Arriving on a distant world, whose ground is composed of papyrus with waterfalls of an ink, Thought finds themself coming face to face with the embodiment they had set their sights on finding.

Dictionary stands at an imposing seven-feet but radiates no threatening aura.

"After all this time, I've finally found you." Thought exclaims.

"Greetings, Thought."

"You know me? How?"

"I know many things, young one," the embodiment replies.

"Are the legends true? Are you the great chronicler, Dictionary?"

"Is that what your generation is calling me now? I am simply *List*. What brings you to my home-world, young Thought?"

"There is an embodiment wreaking havoc on the existence. His domain of influence is one that I believe you have some sway over."

"Who might this embodiment be?" The chronicler asks.

"He goes by Lexicon."

"Ah, Lexicon, tenth to emerge." List says, before raising up her hand. Suddenly, a page of paper from the world flies into her hand. The ink covering the page slowly morphs into writing, which List reads aloud.

"Lexicon is the embodiment of words and within him

resides the power to create any words he may so choose. He may wield words to his liking."

"You know his expression?"

"It is my duty to know. I am the chronicler. On my pages lie record of every embodiment in existence," she says.

"And what of words? I heard stories that you once collected them."

"Modern embodiments tend to emerge given the right word. I chronicle words that could serve that purpose. I know each word's meaning and intention."

"Then it's true that both you and Lexicon deal in words."

"Yes, for different reasons."

"Then you may be able to help!"

"In what way? How has Lexicon wrought havoc?" List asks.

"He is taking words from the mouths and writings of countless worlds."

"Taking words?"

"Yes, it's as if he removes the entire vocabulary from his victims, leaving words unspeakable or writable for anyone he crosses."

"I hadn't noticed. He must not be able to affect my ledger. This is not the kind of behavior I have in my records for Lexicon. Has he gone rogue?"

"That appears to be the case. And it might get worse. Lexicon may attempt to start taking words from embodiments."

"Then this is serious," List says with furrowed brows.

"You see the threat he poses?"

"I do. I can help you, Thought. Recording words is my responsibility. Stopping Lexicon is crucial."

The two embodiments keep speaking, and with that, Thought has completed the task they had set out to do: Finding someone who could put an end to Lexicon's machinations. Thought leaves for the mental-realm, having been away from it for too long and knowing it needed protection, especially in the wake of so many untrained minds now lashing out into existence. List stays in her world for some time, coming up with a plan as to how she will engage Lexicon. But little do either know, there is an embodiment older than both who has been listening to their conversation with interest; one who decides it is now their time to enter the fray.

4 / DEFEND THE EGG

REALITY LISTENS to what Thought says to List, hearing the conversation from the outer edge of space, and finds himself captivated by the information he hears. There is an embodiment out there putting the continuance of existence in jeopardy. Reality did not consider himself a guardian, but found existence to be an intriguing premise from which many interesting occurrences could arise. Intriguing enough that from time to time he felt personally vested in its continued well-being. Space itself was once one of many singularities borne out of a sneeze from Reality. Reality considered himself an occasional ally to existence when it was in need of one. This was one of those moments. Reality would not allow existence to be put into more danger than it could handle. And so, he takes it upon himself to find this Lexicon and deal with his threat.

Unlike Thought who struggled to locate Lexicon, Reality has no such trouble. For Reality, it is only a matter of peering into space from its edge in search of the embodiment he is looking for. When he finds the being who seems to fit the description, roaming within a dark region of space, Reality reaches his arm into the universe, his arm the size of a man's, and simply plucks the embodiment out from the sector of space with a tug at the shoulder. By the time he is finished pulling the personified concept out of space, the embodiment rests in Reality's now unquantifiably large palm. From the living concept's eyes, Reality is a gargantuan of near incomprehensible size and more paramount than the entirety of space beside them. The embodiment in Reality's palm, no taller than the average human, may as well be the size of an electron compared to the hand he has found himself in.

Surrounding both is a vista of permuting colors that aren't of any recognizable spectrum of light the embodiment has ever seen before. New words spring to Lexicon's mind while staring at them. The vista seems to boast zero gravity-like properties as massive platforms litter its expanse, floating through the air and forming walkable pads of ground. Reality sets down Lexicon from his palm so that he floats in front of Reality like an airborne speck of dust, as Reality decreases in size so that he can face the lexical threat eye to eye.

"Who are you, and where are we?" Lexicon asks.

"I am Reality. And perhaps for the first time in your life, you currently reside outside of space. This place is an outer-versal region of existence."

"Outside of space... I didn't know that was possible. I never imagined reality had a face either."

"Not many ever see it. But for you, I made a special exception."

"And why might that be?" Lexicon asks.

"For the trouble you have been causing with your actions across worlds."

"I don't recall committing any acts worth labeling trouble," he replies.

"I know who you are, Lexicon, you are the embodiment

of words. And you taking these words has wrought havoc upon civilizations and risks the destabilization of all."

"You're watching me?"

"Embodiments talk, Lexicon. I listen. Your actions have left a trail that not only I have chosen to follow. Do you have anything to say for yourself?"

"Sure. Any beings whose words I've taken away had it coming. They abuse words just to manipulate each other. And as the embodiment of words, it's my place to decide what goes best for words. I've decided they're better off with me," the embodiment of words explains.

"The rest had their chance. They can learn to come up with something different if they want to communicate with each other, but I won't let anyone tarnish words any longer," he continues.

"And that includes embodiments?"

"I'm still letting you speak now, aren't I?"

"And when you decide otherwise?"

"That will be my choice to make," Lexicon states.

"You realize that in your taking of words, you are also taking the chance for embodiments of that namesake to emerge?"

"If that is the sacrifice that must be made to protect words, then it is one that I am willing to bear the burden of."

"You would weigh words over the continuance of our race?" Reality challenges.

"Of course I would! Words are everything to me!" Lexicon shouts.

"And what of existence? You must know that it will crumble without the continued emergences of embodiments?"

"I didn't ask to emerge. But when I did, letters were my first companions, words my muse. I embody them and they complete me. I would sooner watch existence burn than live in it if words are not treated with their due respect. Perhaps my taking of will be a lesson to appreciate them for the gift that they are."

"I acknowledge your turmoil Lexicon, but seizing words from everyone is not a solution to the underlying issue of disposition, which is what causes living beings to resort to actions such as abusing words. Who is to say they won't just do the same thing with whatever replacement for words they come up with?"

"That won't be my problem. Words are my domain. I alone decide their fate. And I have decided they do not benefit from being used by savages who would only seek to wield them for hatred."

"I don't approve of the way in which certain beings deny their reality," Reality says, "yet I realize they do not degrade the overall quality of reality I have made. You must understand the same for words. Existences are free to make blunders, that is the nature of things. Accepting them for the flaws they bring means you give them the opportunity to produce beauty from their follies."

"I will craft all the beauty words need. They can't even understand the importance of the words that they create. How could I let them keep a word like 'free' if all they do is subjugate each other?"

"You took *free* from them?"

"I felt it necessary."

"*Free* is what is necessary. Do you realize what you've done? You've taken the freedom to express freedom from beings. Restricting the word means you have locked away an aspect of freedom itself. It's very name. And without all aspects of freedom unconstrained, nothing is truly free. The embodiment who personifies what you've taken away in that word must have become trapped by your taking of the word from them. That, is already one pillar of existence put into peril by your actions."

"Existence has continued nonetheless. I am not giving back the words I have taken. They are finally safe with me. I will not return them to a world that will defile them."

"Even so, I can't let you keep holding words back from existence. You can find another way to protect them. The danger posed by your taking of words is too great."

"Then it appears we have come to an impasse."

"It does. Know that I am not the only embodiment intent on retrieving words from you, though."

"I'll have to keep that in mind when I get back to my place in the universe."

"You speak as if I'd let you go, while you still refuse to give back all that you've taken."

"I wasn't making a request."

At that moment, Lexicon wields the word *return*, which appears as a word under his eye, returning him to where he had been removed from. Lexicon's body fades as the spot of space Reality had plucked Lexicon from begins to glow.

"You aren't going anywhere." Reality rebuts, as his gaze meets the glowing spot of space until the color fades, causing Lexicon to reappear as if he had never left.

"Space existed within me long enough that I know how to pull things out of it when necessary, even when separated from me as it is now. You're not getting back into The Egg without my approval."

"I'll only tell you once. Put me back where you took me from."

"Not until I am sure existence is safe from your menace."

"The only safety you should be worrying about is your own, if you don't send me back."

"That sounded like a threat, Lexicon."

"It was. I can make you comply. By force if necessary."

"You can try," Reality says.

Lexicon throws his fist. It connects with Reality's cheek, jerking his face to the side. For a moment, Reality remains motionless, before he turns his head back to his opponent, a slight smirk on his face.

Reality waves one of the hands lowered at his sides and the universe disappears from their sight.

"Is that your plan? To scare me into submitting?" Reality asks.

Reality head-butts Lexicon with blinding speed, meeting Lexicon's forehead with his own. Lexicon staggers back, hands clasping the spot that has just been attacked before replying to Reality, perceivably angered.

"It doesn't look like you'll make this easy for me. In that case, I'll have to bleed you dry until you're forced to bring space back," he mutters.

"Come then. I'll put an end to your threat right here and now." Reality replies, loud and curt.

Both embodiments ready themselves into combat stances. They stare each other down with an overwhelming intensity before Lexicon lunges back, still facing Reality, and places his right hand onto his opposite bicep, his left arm outstretched toward Reality. Wielding the word *rend*, which appears on his left palm, razor sharp gusts of wind begin to burst from Lexicon's hand, marked at Reality. The gusts rip at the very air between the embodiments as they travel. The gusts never meet their mark as Reality maneuvers between each and every one coming towards him. Reality looks up to Lexicon floating above him, still readied in his combat stance.

"Tch." Lexicon grouses.

The word *burn* etches itself across Lexicon's forehead, as flames erupt from his mouth, sent down towards Reality. The flames engulf Reality, who throws his arms in front of himself to meet them. Fire spews from Lexicon in a continuous stream, steadily growing hotter as it comes down on Reality, shifting from a dull red hue, through yellow-white, to a final deep blue. Through the inferno, Reality maintains his defense, smoke billowing around him. Lexicon maintains his fiery assault, until a loud popping noise erupts from the smoke cloud. Satisfied, the fire pouring from Lexicon's mouth simmers down, as the word *burn* slowly dissipates from his forehead. Smirking now, Lexicon watches the plume of smoke masking Reality intently, ready to see the damage his flames have inflicted upon his combatant. When the smoke clears, Reality hovers unscathed, a barrier of energy in front of his arms protecting him. The side of the energy barrier which had faced the oncoming fire bubbling from the heat of Lexicon's attack, but holding steady. Reality lets the barrier dissolve, before going on the offensive.

Reality personified a self-generating framework within existence, internally assembling, in the sense that reality only needed to rely on realness itself to arise. Reality developed as Reality saw it fit to. This gave Reality a certain level of proficiency when it came to generating outcomes, so long as what he generated was internally-consistent with reality's own limits. It was how Reality produced an energy barrier: by generating it, within the boundaries of reality's laws of energy conservation, Reality having converted the air molecules in front of himself into a high-energy wall. One of the properties of reality, was that it provided the underlying structure for any matter to be built upon. Reality could generate whatever underlying structure he could imagine, and matter would respond by being built to that structure's specification. Without matter, Reality still capable of warping any reality he could generate.

Reality stretches out his hand towards Lexicon as a cage materializes around the verbal scourge. Punching one of the bars of the cage, Lexicon is surprised that he doesn't so much as make a dent to it. Reality floats up towards the confined Lexicon: "Stop this now, and we can figure out another way for you to protect words, or I'll have to beat the decency into you."

"I'm getting sick of hearing you use them when you can't understand why my taking of them is for their benefit. You've spoken your last piece!"

"You're making a mista-" Reality never finishes the sentence. He is unable to. Having the words taken from him feels as though an essential piece of himself has just been stripped away. The word *boom* flashes across Lexicon's chest, and suddenly an explosive force emanates from his body carrying a pulverizing concussive force. The explosion tears through the cage surrounding Lexicon and throws Reality backwards through the air until he crashes into one of the massive platforms littering the vista. Slamming his fist into the side of the platform he landed on, Reality dislodges himself from its side, a vicious smile across his face. Reality wouldn't admit it, but he reveled in combat. It was never his first resolve, but it was his favorite. He especially enjoyed the encounters he had with other embodiments which turned fierce, such as the one before him. Reality could no longer speak, but if he could've, his last statement before lunging himself into battle with Lexicon would've been *Fine.*

Reality launches himself off the platform aimed for Lexicon, knuckles clenched. His fist glows with energy as he soars toward Lexicon, prepared to deliver a charged blow to the embodiment in front of him. From Lexicon's position, he floats ready to meet the foe hurtling towards him. Wielding the word *freeze*, which appears across his knuckles and the back of his hand, Lexicon releases five torrents of blue substance from his fingertips that fuse into a cylindrical beam that speeds toward Reality. Placing his left arm in front of himself to meet it, Reality braces the beam as he inches ever closer to Lexicon. When Reality arrives in front of Lexicon's he unleashes an energized right fist on Lexicon, punching him in the gut and sending a shockwave through the outerversal region. While Lexicon reels, Reality continues his assault, landing a kick to Lexicon's side before throwing an elbow down onto the threat's head, sending Lexicon hurtling directly downwards into Reality's knee.

The word *away* appears on Lexicon's back and Lexicon is forcibly pulled one-hundred feet back. Lexicon heaves, a repeating stream of the word blood coming down the side of his mouth. Reality holds up his left arm, frozen inside of a block of ice, and chops at the block of ice with renewed energy, snapping it in two and freeing the hand rendered inert by the effects of Lexicon's *freeze* beam.

Wiping the stream of the word *blood* from his face, Lexicon retakes his combat stance, now committed to bringing down Reality through whatever means necessary. The word *poison* etches itself across his cheek, and like vapor, a purple cloud begins to pour from Lexicon's nose blowing toward his enemy. Reality watches the misty apparition snake toward him. Raising one hand while allowing the other to thaw, Reality gives structure to the air in front of him and hardening it into a wieldable construct, captures the cloud of poison. Reality holds the cloud in hardened air as he works to diffuse it by mixing it with as much air outside the construct as he can conduct. After a few seconds, the cloud soon disperses into the vista.

Lexicon takes the moment to strike. Descending upon him from above, word tendrils shoot out from Lexicon's arm catching Reality in their grip. Lexicon reels him, pulling him into close combat. Lexicon delivers blow after blow to Reality's face while holding him in place with the tendrils. Reality's head buckles, until one of the punches completely throws his head back so that his neck exposes itself to the onslaught. Lexicon strangles him and as he does, flies towards one of the many platforms littered across the vista, slamming Reality straight through it, coming out the other side still holding him by the neck. The word *Flight* plastered on Lexicon's achilles tendon the entire fight. Struggling to free himself from the tendrils and choke hold, Reality enlarges his physique to behemothic stature, snapping the tendrils.

Striking Lexicon with a fist the size of his body, Reality thrusts his opposer directly into another smaller, floating platform roughly two kilometers out. It shatters completely and Reality follows in aerial pursuit, Lexicon floating on his back in between the debris and platform he'd been propelled into. Catching up to Lexicon, Reality delivers an axe kick which connects with Lexicon's supine frame, sending him flying downwards until he hits the colorful edge of the outerversal region's vista. He bounces off it, only for Reality to smash his body back into the edge once more breaking him through it as if piercing out from the inside of a bubble. On the other side, being greeted to a sprawling vascular world of wheeling interconnected threads. Lexicon crashes into one of the threads and is spun around and thrown into another large thread, wheeling the opposite direction. Lexicon hits the thread prone. Arms and legs sprawled. He stands up against its localized gravity. He looks up; a still giant, but now only colossally sized Reality falls towards him. Lexicon runs with the direction of the turning thread. On his shoulder running down, the word *Spark*. Lexicon points his arm up towards Reality, and using a significant portion of his stamina, discharges bolts of electric light at him with enough energy to momentarily illuminate galaxies. The bolts meet their mark, and Reality sparks. Shouting in pain, a now fractured Reality descends, for the first time harmed. A single shard of erratic element dislodges itself from Reality's frame, and like a bolt of lightning, splinters with unfathomable dynamism before warping itself out of the battlefield.

———

Time just watches, sitting atop a temporally static thread in the distance.

Possibility appears.

"Looks like I made it," she huffs a deep breath, as if she is just arriving after a long journey.

"This must be what called me here," she says, witnessing the raging battle from a far-off vantage point in the air.

Awestruck for a moment by the sheer mayhem generated by the two embodiments, as they break through tapestries of threads in the height of their battle. Possibility quickly snaps herself back to focus.

"I should get to work."

Holding out her hand, Possibility extends her influence into a multi-kilometer-wide perimeter around the battlefield, surrounding the battling embodiments and the network of wheeling threads within their proximity. As the fighters maneuver through the weaving threads, Possibility's influence follows, keeping the two embodiments confined within its boundaries even as they move and fight.

"There. That should do it," Possibility says, satisfied with her execution.

"You just did something interesting, didn't you?," Time says, standing on another once-wheeling thread floating next to Possibility.

"Who are you? The possibility of anyone other than me being called to this event was astronomically low."

"Ah, I suppose this is *sooner* than we were originally supposed to meet. I am Time."

"Time... I didn't think I'd be running into any embodiments to chat with here. If this is *sooner* than we originally meet like you say, then this must be the past for you, right?"

"Quite perceptive. This isn't exactly the same past as I once knew, though."

"What are you doing here, then?"

"You could say I took a gamble, which seems to have brought me to this moment... I'm merely here to observe, though. What you are here for seems to be of much more pressing importance."

"It is."

"And for what, pray-tell, may that be?"

"Why would I tell you?" Possibility bites.

"That's right, I haven't yet earned your trust at this point."

"You say that like you're sure you will."

"I did."

"Maybe back in your old future. But not with me now."

"No, not with you indeed."

Possibility floats silently, as she scrutinizes Time.

"... I'm surrounding the fight with... possibility."

"You're telling me?"

"The possibility of me being able to trust you is high. I can just tell that kind of thing."

"That's a relief. Would you care to explain why you're doing that?"

"I suppose not. I appear *where the outcome of events is legitimately indeterminable*. When that happens, I am called to infuse the event with possibilities so that the undetermined outcome becomes one of many *possible* outcomes. This fight must be one of an indeterminable outcome, which is why it called to me. Therefore, I've surrounded it with possibilities until it concludes, so that one possible outcome may be reached. Adjacently, existence has a risk of tearing when an indeterminable event goes on for too long," Possibility explains.

"Interesting. I wonder what this outcome will be?" Time ponders, as they watch the two embodiments brawl from within the influence of untempered possibility.

"We'll have to wait and see. At this point, the probabilities for how this could go are as sprawling as this place," she says, gesturing to the vast setting they find themselves in.

"I have time."

"I usually leave after I've accomplished the mission," she says, looking at the battlefield her influence extends over. "But I guess I can stick around for a while longer here."

Possibility takes a seat next to Time on the static thread. They both watch as the fight continues between the two forces ahead of them.

THE WORD *LAUNCH* ETCHES ACROSS LEXICON'S LEFT LEG, AND Lexicon leaps through the air, bounding between wheeling threads as he evades swipes from Reality's palms - now only as large as Lexicon's upper-body. In a final leap the word *launch* dissipates from Lexicon's leg, and is just as quickly replaced by the word *brawn,* which flashes against Lexicon's back. Lexicon's muscles bulge, gaining Olympian mass, as he soars towards Reality's face. Pulling back his now excessively brawny arm, Lexicon strikes. His fist meets Reality's in a magnitudinous clash, inducing a shockwave that ripples through their surroundings, blowing apart threads in every direction. Lexicon is flung backwards, and lands between a web of half-snapped threads, not wheeling. He heaves, the word blood flowing from each of his grazed knuckles.

Reality hovers in the air, still in the same position, jostling his hand, shaking off the monumental impact of the blow he just delivered, fractures still present across the length of his body. He glances up towards the immobile Lexicon and flies towards him.

Incapable of freeing himself from the threads in time, Lexicon improvises. The word *drown* appears on Lexicon's neck, and seconds before Reality reaches his position, a flood of water is expelled from Lexicon's mouth, nose, ears, and every other pore of his body, creating a tsunami that envelops Reality and takes the shape of a gigantic sphere of water around him. Watching Reality struggle from within the sphere, Lexicon smiles.

Embodiments didn't need to breathe. But using a word like *drown*, Lexicon hoped he could force the concept on Reality.

To his dismay, he witnesses the water surrounding Reality transform into vapor. From within the aqueous containment sphere, Reality has his arms extended, using his mastery over the underlying structure of matter to desta-bilize the intermolecular attraction between the particles of water around him, causing the water to convert into gas. After only several seconds, the containment sphere is completely evaporated by Reality, who opens his mouth letting out piping hot steam as he floats between the threads Lexicon just escaped from. Even the wetness still clinging to his body soon dissipates into steam. That's when bullets of verbal sweat start running down Lexicon's forehead.

Lexicon mounts his next offensive, desperately; the word *blast* inscribed on his arm. Emanating from his palms, projectiles in the shape of letters burst towards Reality at high-speed like guided missiles. At his size, Reality is too large to dodge all of the blasts. Reality takes blows from the projectiles, which throw him backwards. As he tumbles through the air, Reality shrinks in size, back down to a humanoid level just taller than Lexicon to better avoid the lettered projectiles. As Reality flies between threads evading projectiles, energy radiates from his fingertips. Aiming his hands forward then, Reality counters Lexicon's blasts with his own beams of energy. A chase ensues during their shooting match; Lexicon runs and jumps along the lengths of moving threads while Reality pursues him mid-flight. Producing a higher output of beams than Lexicon can expel blasts, one of Reality's beams hits Lexicon, knocking him off his feet and lodging him into the ground of one of the threads. Swooping down, Reality delivers an energy charged blow to Lexicon's stomach, knocking him through one thread straight down into another.

Still on his back, reacting to Reality's descent, Lexicon grips the thread beneath him to both sides of his head, throwing himself into a backwards handspring, thrusting him to his feet just far back enough to avoid Reality's crashing fist. Not missing a beat, the word *twister* spreads itself just above Lexicon's upper lip, while he blows air out of his mouth. Quickly, the air wraps around itself, picking up current, forming a whirlwind aimed at Reality.

Reality leaps backwards taking evasive flight. Soon, Lexicon's blow produces three large tornados, which continually redirect their trajectory as they chase Reality around the vascular thread-system. Maneuvering around threads as he flies, Reality can't shake the now four twisters following him. Reality soars upwards just before one of the twisters reaches his position. To his misfortune however, the three other twisters, anticipating his path, converge on his spot. Reality is enveloped by the twisters, which merge into one super tornado, and carried by its immense thrust whirling through threads which get caught in its spin.

The threads caught in the tornado become deadly

whips, which strike Reality as he is held by the tornado's grip. The fractures on Reality's body deepen as he is dragged by the tornado and lashed by the thick threads. With the only coherency he has left all he can do is scream in pain. Finding enough balance to hold himself upright through the chaos of the tornado's spin, Reality curls himself into a ball, as energy charges around his entire body. Extending his limbs into a full-stretch Reality expels a tremendous amount of energy in a massive omnidirectional outburst, which completely destabilizes the tornado enveloping him.

Lexicon, having taken vantage on one of the threads near Reality during the tornado's rage, unloads a massive cone-shaped soundwave toward the embodiment in a banshee wail, the word *sonics* etched under his bottom lip. The soundwave hits Reality with a concentrated force enough to pulverize Jupiter, blasting him hundreds of meters down until he hits a patch of threads, weaved together so that they form a wide flat ground. Jumping down to meet him, Lexicon continues to bellow out high-decibel soundwaves which strike Reality incessantly, keeping him pinned to the flat weave of threads. Resisting the conical wave of sound, Reality stretches out his arm and materializes a sound-proof cube around Lexicon. Try as he might, none of Lexicon's wails make any success in breaching the sound-proof walls of the cube around him. In fact, as Lexicon wails at the interior of the cube, his vocal emanations only bounce back against the edges of the cube and strike Lexicon himself. Lexicon's pain and subsequent loss of focus prompts Reality to notice one thing: That his ability to use words has returned. As Lexicon bangs on the walls of the cube with his fists, Reality walks towards the trapped embodiment, ready to end this conflict.

The word *disintegrate* appears on Lexicon's hand, firing a red ray from his palm, which reduces one of the walls of the cube to its constituent atoms. Exiting the cube then, Lexicon fires the rays at Reality, as he shouts "I'll leave just as much reality as I need to make finding Space simple!"

Flying in an erratic pattern, Reality avoids Lexicon's rays, and speaking to himself, declares: "This is getting dangerous. I should get serious."

Swooping in low, Reality delivers an uppercut to Lexicon's jaw that thrusts Lexicon up into the air before Reality grabs one of Lexicon's legs from below and spins him into a throw sending him dozens of feet away. Landing on his back, Lexicon grunts in pain as Reality continues to soar towards him. Predicting the path Reality's flight will take, Lexicon aims his palm up towards the air, and fires a disintegration ray. Noticing the telegraph of Lexicon's aim before firing, Reality still meets the path of the disintegration ray, and is hit on one of his arms. Lexicon watches as the ray hits Reality, his arm breaking down before Lexicon's eyes. Lexicon continues to fire disintegration rays with his advantage claimed, and the rays hit Reality on his right leg, left calf, and head, which all disintegrate in the process. To be sure he has won, Lexicon fires a final two disintegration rays at the floating remains of Reality's body, hitting his chest and thigh of his left leg. Leaving only Reality's left arm floating in the air.

Laughing, Lexicon approaches the left arm, ready to claim his prize for defeating Reality, when a kick smacks his head that sends him flying meters back onto the weaved ground of threads. Floating where the kick was just delivered, is a leg, and a slowly materializing body to go with it, culminating in the reformation of Reality, body now completely free of any fractures. A frenzied look on Reality's face. When Lexicon looks towards where the floating left arm should be, it is gone, however.

"I disintegrated you... How are you still here?" Lexicon questions.

"Reality materializes and it can dematerialize too." Reality boldly states, leaving his explanation open-ended.

"Let's see how you deal with this, then!" Lexicon shouts, revealing his trump-card.

The word *win* burns itself across Lexicon's forehead, and suddenly Reality finds himself bombarded by a combination of all the prior word-effects Lexicon has used during their fight. Fire, lightning, frozen beams, cloud-like poison, high-energy sonics, and blasts in the shape of words all strike Reality simultaneously. Suddenly, the spot where he is floating erupts in a fatal explosion. Using words such as *burn* or *freeze* is a simple matter for Lexicon, but using open-ended words such as *win* gives him more trouble, as the literal reaction from wielding the word would need to be distilled into a concrete effect. For the effect of *win* Lexicon called upon; re-initiating all of the prior words he had wielded during their fight; taking a brutal toll on the rest of Lexicon's stamina. Though content washes over him, as he stares at an utterly ravaged Reality lying motionless on the ground before him.

"It's over," Lexicon says, walking towards the body on the ground in front of him. "Time to go home."

The word *return* once again appears under Lexicon's eye, and a spot on Reality's left arm starts glowing,

"I guess he kept it close right till the end," Lexicon muses as he

vanishes into space, housed within Reality's left arm. Where Lexicon reappears, however, he is not met with the same realm of space from which he came.

"You couldn't have thought it would be that easy for you," a voice calls out to Lexicon.

Lexicon looks up to find Reality, domineering above him as the fractures in his body slowly start to heal.

"How...? I watched my attack ravage you."

"Not the original me," Reality asserts.

"Original you?"

"That was an Alternate Reality you just attacked. You didn't notice how the damage you did to me wasn't present in the newfound reality, did you?"

"But when could you have swapped yourself out?"

"I didn't say which Reality rematerialized after facing your disintegration ray, did I?"

"The arm..." Lexicon hesitates.

"I could tell you were going all out, so I let an Alternate Reality take my place while I recuperated. In fact, you're in an alternate reality right now, and there are more of those where that came from." Reality continues.

Suddenly, five of him all materialize around Lexicon, each brandishing facial expressions as dissimilar as the color wheel.

"You did well enough against me. But now let's see how you fare against multiple Realities."

The Realities swarm Lexicon and unleash a torrent of energized punches and kicks that knock Lexicon into the next consecutive attack continuously. Lexicon wails in pain amidst their onslaught. The word *escape* inscribes itself on Lexicon's back, but in his suffering he once again loses sight of his focus.

From within the confines of Possibility's multi-kilometer wide *infusion of possibility*, the right conditions for a single possibility to become the definitive outcome between the pair are met.

Lexicon planned on using the word *escape* to get out of the beating he had found himself in, but in his loss of focus, the *possibility* emerged that his usage of *escape* might result in an outcome completely different than what he had intended. Thanks to the sphere of possibilities surrounding Lexicon and Reality, that *possibility* of an unintended application of *escape* becomes definite. The now confirmed possibility was that the word *escape* Lexicon wielded, would apply; but to a subject other than Lexicon himself. What that amounted to was an escape being made, but not for the one who needed it most.

The word inscribed on Lexicon's back warps until it separates itself from his skin and floats into the air above. Lexicon continues to receive blows from each Alternate Reality. The floating word *escape* begins to fold into itself until it fissures into a portal from whose opening a voice emerges:

"Lexicon? Is that you?"

"NO!" Lexicon shouts between taking punches, knowing the escape just made above him does not apply to him.

"That is you. But I can feel this. It's a way out," the voice continues.

The orifice begins to collapse in on itself.

"You can't hold me in here much longer. I'll be free, then everyone will!"

The portal disappears from the alternate reality Lexicon and the Realities find themselves in.

Reality's eyes widen as he watches on from a distance, having seen into the portal himself. Reality then snaps his fingers, and he, Lexicon, and the Alternate Realities are transported back to the weaved ground of threads of the vascular region, beside the Alternate Reality that Lexicon entered just prior when he thought he was re-entering Space. Reality lifts his arm, and the five Alternate Realities engaged in combat with Lexicon halt their attacks. Lexicon falls to the threaded ground, bloodied by the beating.

"We can stop fighting now. It's over." Reality says.

"Not until I get back to where you took me from," Lexicon replies, as he clammers to his feet.

"I saw into that rift. It came from the *escape* you conjured. I think I understand your expression. Whatever word you employ becomes a literal phenomenon. That must mean the rift itself was an escape created by you."

Lexicon doesn't reply but his facial expression tells Reality everything he needs to know.

"But it wasn't an escape for you, was it? You didn't sound very happy about that rift opening up. Almost as if it shouldn't have," Reality continues.

"Stop talking."

"I know where the rift ended up, even now. It returned to a place within space. As long as I make sure you don't get to it, with just a little time, I'm positive *he'll* get out of the captivity you put him into."

"Why aid someone you have no obligation to?"

"He said once he was free, everyone else would be too. I can only assume he meant free of your tyranny over words. There could only be one existence who could make that happen. Freedom. That is someone who I would willingly lend my assistance to."

"You can't keep me here forever."

"No. I suppose I can't. However, I can keep you out of space for as long as it takes for Freedom to escape and return the sovereignty of communication to all."

"Then you're no better than me for taking words."

"No, Lexicon. The difference between us is that I'm keeping you out of space to give existence a fighting shot. And now that escape has been made for someone who might be able to liberate people's constrictions, that shot is possible. You taking words is only an offense that puts existence in danger."

"Watch how you speak to me Reality. You only have

words with my permission."

"And I can fight you until you can't keep holding them back from me. You're in no position to threaten me."

"Perhaps you can fight for your words, but the rest can't. No matter what you do, I'll still have their words whether I'm in space or not."

"That's why I'm trusting that Freedom can help free people of you once he escapes from that rift. I understand that you feel it necessary to protect words at any cost. Just as you should understand that my confronting you is for the sake of existence. "

"Then we were bound to fight here."

"I could wipe you out right now with a wave or a glance. But I don't hate you Lexicon. In fact, I'm not opposed to you returning to space, eventually. I just need to be sure the threat you pose to existence has been neutralized. I can't let you continue to wreak havoc within space. When I do allow you back into it, measures will have been taken to prevent you from taking words ever again. The escape of Freedom is now one of them."

"And how do you intend to keep me from trying to enter space?"

Reality gestures to the five Alternate Realities standing around them.

"They'll be keeping you company while I make sure space is somewhere you won't be able to easily find it."

The Alternate Realities assume combat stances. One poses while balanced on his fingertip.

"How violent they become depends only on what you do."

Lexicon points at the Alternate Reality he bombarded with attacks when he wielded the word *win*. It is slowly dissipating.

"If that one's anything to go by, I might be able to make short work of them."

"You'll just have to see about that for yourself. As entertaining as it was fighting you Lexicon, I bore of this scenery. I'm leaving. Try to reconsider your actions while you're stuck here."

"I'll find you."

"You won't have to. You can re-enter space if you can find it, without worry about my interference once I know words have begun to return to everyone you've taken them from. And for that to begin, all I have to do is wait until Freedom escapes from your entrapment. Goodbye. I'll be listening."

And with that, Reality warps, and vanishes, leaving Lexicon standing in the threaded vascular region surrounded by five Alternate Realities.

Lexicon breaks the silence between them.

"It's going to be a long way until I'm home."

He readies himself.

The words *recharge* and *enhance* appear on Lexicon's arms as his entire body bulges in size and his wounds slowly begin to heal.

The Alternate Reality on its fingertip pulls out its tongue just as Lexicon lunges.

5 / STANLEY PARABLE

On Earth, havoc grips the population who cannot so much as articulate their anguish. Reduced to supreme incoherency, society struggles to organize itself in any way comparable to the eloquence of using words. The most people can do is express their most basic feelings through gestures, body language, and facial expressions. With words stolen, actions like writing or typing are impossible, either never appearing at all, or the letters deconstructing to their most primordial iterations before blipping from sight.

Few appreciate just how essential words are until they don't have the- anymore. If humanity had gone far in its advancement, it was through the benefits of community; the removal of words, humanity's lexicon, their means of communication; a sentencing nothing short of cataclysmic. The inability to communicate with someone due to a lack of language comprehension is torturous. This is far worse.

Without words, the world's population are forced mute, unable to so much as even attempt dialogue between each other. All stored knowledge is lost, the words simply vanished from the pages they were written. Productivity is incapable of thriving, much less surviving, as workers cannot speak to each other, leaving every major industry crippled. Energy is the first major industry to collapse worldwide, whose loss massively reverberates through society. Without the words to coordinate the running of power-stations, the Earth is plunged into a blackout of its highest historic severity.

Transport is quickly lost. The blow of that quickly costs the planet too many lives. People with spare generators slowly run on fumes as they use up their power. Only those savvy enough to have invested in renewable energy like solar or wind power are able to maintain a steady supply of electrical power in their homes for the time being. For everyone else, they are abandoned to a dark-age without the resources to generate their homes. Within the first week of words removed, there is a grievous rise in theft and looting with no way for those who have been stolen from to tell anyone who stole from them, or even that they had been stolen from at all. It's every family for themselves. Neighbors, friends, and clusters of people who manage to find each other huddle together for safety. They survive by scavenging the stores in their local areas and by pooling together any resources they have left.

All means of mass-media communication are debilitated. Without words radio loses its use, television simply becomes an assortment of silent videos on channels that still run, and news cycles are hollowed out as no words are available to render daily reports. In this wordless world, other mediums become essential to do the talking for humans. In fact, there are four comprehensible sources capable of conveying any information left, and they do so through imagery, iconography, charades, and with numbers. Of those four mediums however, only three are really viable. Despite the massive collection of images that are available or stored on databases, resources such as the internet become gated-off, as users are unable to make use of the search function without a way to type the words out.

Stanley steps out of the house. Last week he lost the dice roll and today, he drew the short straw. It's his turn to go out and scavenge for the group. With Stanley now gone, four friends are left to occupy the fortress that was once their home. He'll have to find enough food for the five of them tonight, and their supplies are running short. Stanley leaves with eight dollars in hand, pooled together from the findings of his group the prior week. It'll have to do. Money has become increasingly tight ever since the word loss.

Yet six distinct words are the only ones left in store: I'll... Take... Your... Word... For... It... remain the last words still written in any form on Earth. Not many collectives even have the assortment of books or written material necessary to unravel the complete message, but Stanley's group does. They cannot discuss it, but every member wordlessly acknowledges that *something* caused words to disappear, and that the phrase *I'll take your word for it* had something to do with it.

Stanley rounds the second corner on his house's street. He's taking a route he knows. Above, the sky resonates a deep innocent blue. Looking up as he walks, Stanley is enthralled by the gentle stride of clouds basking across the horizon. His eyes transfix on one in particular– its shape is unmistakable. Had this been any other era of humanity, Stanley would've been enamored with the cloud. But right now, all it does is taunt him. And on such a beautiful day, Stanley lets it. He makes an attempt at saying the word describing the cloud outloud. Of his group, Stanley still tries to verbalize the most. Before he can mouth the first phoneme of the word, a familiar pang reverberates through his throat. He hates the feeling, it visits him every time he tries to say something, anything...

"Nramn" he mumbles. "Mrmon," he tries again, this time the pang in his throat growing to an ache.

"Drgahhh!" Stanley cries, clutching at his neck, throbbing in pain. This is his limit. He simply cannot articulate the word he wants to say. His body won't let him. It is as if the word is simply barred from leaving his mouth. All at once, the dragon-shaped cloud loses its outline, turning amorphous, and Stanley lowers his head in defeat, unable to quell the despair he feels in his inability to expel even a single word. For several weeks now that's how it's been for any word he has tried to utter. Only grunts or mumbles coming through, but never the word he hoped to say. Stanley continues his scavenger-hunt for food in silence, taking the third right along the boulevard.

Stanley arrives at his destination, the local supermarket. In the weeks since word loss first happened, the store has been raided countless times, the store owner quickly scrounging together what funds she had to hire two guards who now stand at the entrance of the store. Stanley wonders how the store owner could've managed to employ these guards without being able to speak, but he finally settles on the thought that it was probably a combination of knowing them prior to the loss, and the ability to flash money in their faces. It was baffling to Stanley that money still functioned comfortably even given the circumstances. He thought the store owner was lucky the two guards hadn't just robbed her on the spot, which led him to conclude that she probably had a stash of money hidden somewhere.

Why those guards were there was besides the point for Stanley, however. He had a mission he was here to complete and that was to find food for his companions. He didn't have the time to stand around and dwell because he knew that if night fell while he was still outside, he'd be at a much higher risk of meeting raiders or scavengers. The world had become a dark, cruel place since words were lost. People robbed and stole to survive. Not Stanley or his group though. At least not yet.

Stanley walks in between the two guards standing at the face of the supermarket. They silently pat him down before allowing him entrance to the store *once deeming him a non-threat.* One of the guards allows Stanley entrance into the store while the other brandishes a pistol and provides cover for his partner, making sure no bandits reveal themselves to make an attempt at the supermarket. When Stanley makes it through the entrance to the store, the guards behind him seal the door, and with a loud click, Stanley hears the door lock behind him.

In front of him extends the sprawling interior to the supermarket. Its lights are still working which tells Stanley that there is likely a spare generator or some form of renewable energy in use somewhere. To every side stands shelves packed halfway full of cereals, juices, breads and snacks. Walking through the aisles, Stanley makes his way to the meat section.

While words are gone, numbers aren't. Stanley looks at a slab of beef. With the gas stove still functional back home and the matches and lighter Stanley knew his group of friends had access to, with just a bit of oil, Stanley contemplated splurging on the beef. Looking at the price and appreciating that he can still read and write numbers, he sees the price of meat is labeled as a solid 6, the dollar currency implicit.

This is much more expensive than he had anticipated, easily the highest price for a pound of beef Stanley had ever seen. With only eight dollars to his group's name, Stanley grits his teeth while staring at the abomination. The store owner must be up-charging, a gutsy thing to do when people are on the verge of starvation and death. With food becoming more and more scarce though, there wasn't much one could do but accept the bogus prices.

"Augh," Stanley scoffs, as he could still do that at least, before continuing his way through the store in search of a more affordable sustenance. He is irked by the high price of the beef, but he isn't furious. His group has a vegetarian, well, a lapsing vegetarian, who tried her best not to eat meat when it could be helped, so Stanley didn't feel pressured to bring meat back to his group. He could just opt for a fully vegetarian-friendly platter for his friends tonight. Standing in the aisle, Stanley finds a box of pasta with a 3 across it and a small bag of rice for 4. That leaves him with one dollar, and just barely enough food to keep his group's stomachs full for another night or two. They were on the brink of getting desperate. If they couldn't find more money lying around the area, they wouldn't be able to buy any more food. And that scared Stanley, enough to make him act out of character.

As he makes his way to the register he sees the store owner standing behind the counter with a whistle around her neck. She still has her name tag on even though it's blank where her name used to be. People all cope in their own way, Stanley thinks to himself. But Stanley knows her name is Priscilla, after all —they'd gone to high school together. He knows that she inherited the supermarket after her father got sick from cancer, and he knows that she is a single mom to David, a shy six-year-old boy he met once in passing. Stanley would have asked about David now, if only he were able.

Approaching the counter, Priscilla instantly recognizes him and smiles. She offers him a wave and he returns the gesture in kind. Had the words not been stripped from their mouths, they might have struck up a conversation– Priscilla asking about Stanley's family and Stanley asking how David was holding up now that schools and parks were shut down. It would have been a pleasant conversation and suddenly Stanley realizes how much he misses simple pleasantries with strangers in passing.

Little gestures are all they can muster now, and it has to be enough for the both of them. Stanley puts the box of pasta and bag of rice on the counter before him and slides a five dollar note and two one dollar coins toward Priscilla. She silently reads the price tags of each before claiming the money. How sad that they couldn't even utter a word, yet money still spoke between them all the same. Perspiration forms around Stanley's armpits yet Priscilla doesn't notice, she is too preoccupied smiling at the dollar signs in her hands. Owning a supermarket with upscaled prices had to be quite the lucrative business in these trying times.

After a moment she gestures towards the back-door exit of the supermarket. Stanley follows her lead as she unlocks the door and stretches her arm out, pointing out his exit. Their transaction is over. As Stanley heads out the door guilt rattles him, and just before Priscilla goes inside, he turns back and stops the door with his foot.

"Hmm?" The owner inflects.

"Hghgh" Stanley clears his throat, while looking at the ground. He can't look her in the eye.

Raising her arms to her sides and shrugging her shoulders, Priscilla's gesture indicates confusion as to why he turned back. With an shameful sigh Stanley empties his jacket pocket to reveal a can of beans he'd swiped from one of the shelves in passing. He shoves the can of beans into Priscilla's hands before crouching himself to his knees, hands clasped in forgiveness. He simply couldn't reduce himself to the level of a thief.

With a pain in her eyes Stanley has never seen before, Priscilla grabs the whistle around her neck and blows into it with sustained intensity which produces a loud echo through the empty alleyway. Her two guards burst into view from behind Stanley and surround him on either side. One brandishes his gun while the other holds Stanley's arms behind his back. They recognize the whistle as Priscilla's anti-bandit detection-measure and the armed guard points his gun to Stanley's foot before looking back at the store owner. She shakes her head from side to side, and balls one of her hands into a fist, which she thrusts into the can of beans held by her other hand. The guard puts his gun away and begins to lay a beating into Stanley, starting with a swift punch to his gut. Stanley takes repeated blows to the face and falls to the ground, before the guard begins to kick into his ribs.

"GAHH", Stanley reels. Just before the guard prepares to stomp on Stanley's face, he is grabbed by the store owner, who holds him back. Priscilla doesn't look happy, but she nods her head, satisfied. She gestures for the guards to leave, and they do, returning to their post at the front of the store. Stanley lies on the ground heaving, blood trickling through his shirt. He looks up at Priscilla. She meets his gaze with her own and he can see that she is frowning. Stepping forward she bends down to pick up the haul of pasta and rice he dropped, putting them back into the paper bag which now lies on the ground beside him. She slips the can of beans in there too, her gaze locked with his.

Priscilla rises and bows with her arms clasped, in the same way Stanley did when he returned the beans. To Stanley, it looks like she is apologizing and despite the beating, he understands. After all, it's just business. She had to teach him his lesson for trying to steal, but, but he can keep the beans. The act seems to tell him that she needs the item less than she needs the community to take her seriously. And perhaps even fear her. Regardless, the "gift" feels like a gesture of kindness, perhaps for the rapport they once shared. Priscilla returns to the half-closed back door and takes one last opportunity to look back at Stanley. She smiles. The door closes and leaves Stanley writhing on the ground in the alley alone, beaten and bruised...

After a minute of panting and shuffling in pain, Stanley stands up. He grabs the paper bag off of the floor and looks inside it. Good. At least none of the food he bought was damaged and his mission had been successful, almost. Had the bags ripped and the food wasted, Stanley wouldn't have been able to face his group. Now he could return to them proudly, even if someone at home would have to tend to the wounds left across his midsection.

A single car occupies the expanse of the store parking lot. Probably Priscilla's if it's the only one there. If Stanley were closer to the pickup truck, he could make out its brand or model, but being so close to the storefront side of the building where the guards stand, Stanley avoids approaching the vehicle.

Walking back along the roadside, Stanley finds himself in particularly high spirits. Despite the beating, he had accomplished what his group had sent him out to do. None of his friends would have to go hungry tonight and that thought alone energized his mood.

"Haaah." He bellows, expressing his satisfaction through an overjoyed sigh. As he walks he shows appreciation for his surroundings, paying silent respect to the emerald gleam of the grass beside his feet, brightened by the glowing after-noon sun above his head. It's nearing sunset, and a fiery hue paints the horizon leaving dazzling shades of red, orange, and pink in a choir across the maturing sky. All around him, nature brims with life, as insects soar through the air and find their footing on radiant sunflowers and golden daffodils. The sight of a butterfly, with wings of the softest violet, stops Stanley in his tracks. Enthralled by its simplistic beauty, he watches as it lands atop a lone stem of lavender plant. The butterfly stays there for a moment, no doubt enjoying a feast of pollen and nectar, before spreading its wings and flying away.

Stanley bends down and plucks the lavender plant. Words might be gone, but on this day, romance doesn't have to be, as Stanley knows a certain lapsing vegetarian who might appreciate the flower. *This is for Jenn*, he thinks to himself. For prospects of romance and internal thoughts are all he can look forward to in the present moment.

Stanley rounds the corner leading him back onto the boulevard just before his house's street. Sitting on lawn chairs off to the right are two comfortably seated people with objects in their hands. Stanley freezes and slowly begins to back away from the boulevard but it's too late– he's been spotted.

Before Stanley can make a clean escape, one of the two bandits is already sprinting towards him, the other still resting in their lawn chair. Taken aback, Stanley stumbles backwards, tripping over himself. Falling with his back to the ground, Stanley recoils when the bandit reaches him. Looming over Stanley, the bandit extends their arm. Bringing it down slowly, Stanley shuts his eyes and braces for the worst. A hand grabs his arm–

Stanley finds himself being lifted off the ground. When he opens his eyes he is greeted to a smiling face accompanied with long flowing hair and dark eyes. Something about her stirs a slight feeling in him and for once, he's thankful that awkward words can't sway the moment. Stanley goes red in the face as he can now surmise that this is in fact, not the bandit he thought them to be.

She gestures to his hand and points toward the lawn chairs, inviting him to follow. The stranger, a woman who looks like she couldn't be out of her twenties, brings him to the other person still sitting down who promptly nods at Stanley in an unspoken greeting.

Stanley's eyes widen as his eyes land on the objects in front of him, instantly grasping the importance of what is in front of him: photographs and hand-made drawings. Both have become invaluable commodities; the imagery of essentials such as food and water widely sought after.

All one had to do was point to the picture on a page in order to communicate what they needed, and possibly where to find it.

Images ranging from first aid kits to batteries make up the content that the stranger is holding; objects that you wouldn't be able to describe without having the capacity to use words. Cycling through the images in his hands, the young woman stops Stanley when he gets to a drawing of a bottle of water. She presses the tips of her right thumb, index, and middle fingers together while her ring and pinky fingers are clenched into her palm, and she uses her three fingers to touch the drawing, before tapping her collarbone three times. Using the same hand, she begins to scribble at the air with the same three fingers, before looking back at Stanley with pride.

Stanley looks back at her puzzled. Communication without words just as difficult as one might imagine. She repeats the action in the wake of his confusion... They stare at each other hopelessly. Slowly, she takes the same three fingers again and touches the image twice before she begins scribbling in the air. She can see him working out the puzzle of her actions by the expression on his face.

"Aahh," Stanley exhales in acknowledgement.

He points at the drawing and then back to the young woman, his eyes showing sudden bewilderment. She nods, smiling. He understands.

Attached to each image is a number. 3 for the bottle of water, 2 on the loaf of bread: Prices. Why else would he have been dragged to the lawn chairs to look at these images? The two artists were selling pictures which was a clever business venture considering the world's circumstances. He continues to cycle through the assortment of images in his hand and stops when he reaches the drawing of a candle. Without electricity those are certainly valuable. His group only had one or two left and yet he hadn't seen any candles in the supermarket.

Perhaps if he brought the image to Priscilla, she could point him in the direction of somewhere that might have them, maybe even drive him there, provided he pay for her services most likely. He looks at the price tag, 5 it reads, and he sighs. These people really knew how to run someone dry. Stanley looks at the young woman, and points to the drawing as she he removes it from the pile of images in his hand. She mimics the number 5 through splayed fingers.

Stanley pulls out his last dollar and shrugs as if to convey that it's all he's got. In lieu of words, he hopes she can understand.

She does and frowns, shaking her head. 5, she signs out again. How could one hope to haggle when you can't even articulate your discontent at the price of the service given to you? He throws his hands up in a full shrug, and flashes the one at her one last time. She doesn't even acknowledge it. For being so friendly just before, it seems like the unsuccessful transaction has drained her of the affability once there before. Stanley really hated what word loss had done to the people he met. It seemed like all they cared about now was staying alive, which he could understand, and money.

Stanley doesn't feel like entertaining this transaction any longer. It feels pointless with the amount of money he has on hand; he gives the pair a thumbs up and resumes the short journey home. At least he has secured their food and by this time, they are probably starting to feel ravished from hunger.

Stanley hasn't traveled more than a couple feet when he feels a tap on his shoulder. He turns to see the young woman behind him. She sighs and signs out a 1 with her finger, holding the drawing of the candle in her other hand. Stanley smiles. Was he just lucky today, or were people in this age not so bad after all?

They exchange a smile and she turns to leave but before she reaches the lawn chair, there is a tender tap on her shoulder. She turns around to find Stanley there, arm extended holding the lavender and a smile. Her eyes light up and she grasps the flower, breathing in its scent, before embracing him in gratitude. Even though he lost the flower he planned on giving to a certain lapsing vegetarian, he felt that it had gone to the right place. Romance could wait yet another day.

By now it's almost dire that Stanley returns home. With darkness descending there are new prospects of danger looming around every corner. Turning back onto his street, Stanley is stopped by a sight he wouldn't be able to put into words even if he had them. In what can only be described as a swirling mass. No, a swirling lack of mass. Like a gateway. A rift. Hovering just mid-air above him

Something about the apparition terrifies Stanley and he feels his throat start to constrict. He tries to gasp but it's useless, as if the rift is pulling even the last vestiges of articulation from his being. While he can't comprehend why this is appearing before him, his instincts are cause to believe that this *thing* is what's causing humanity's current crisis. And yet, something about the rift calls to him, a spark of hope. A feeling of *freedom* emanating from somewhere inside it.

Stanley takes a step forward toward the rift. He knows he can't reach it, and yet, he finds himself trying anyway. The primal opening responds in turn, slowly descending downwards with each step Stanley takes towards it. As the two come face to face he can see that it is a circular vortex, slightly larger than the size of any human. Blackness swirls as the gyre hovers in place. Through the eye Stanley makes out a sole word, the first he's seen besides the six in weeks. It says: *escape.*

Stanley reaches for the word without thought or hesitation. The feeling of liberation swells around and envelopes him like heavy fleece in the dead of winter. Something tells him that if can just get through that rift, this nightmare will end. And yet somehow he's managed to forget about everyone at home; he's forgotten about the food, the candle, the day's events and just about anything of reason. What calls to him now is whatever lies within this rift- beckoning him, pulling him into it- he gets closer and closer and prepares to absorb himself into the gyrating mass.

"Stop," a voice sounds and everything freezes in place. Birds float suspended in the air. Leaves being carried by the wind become stagnant and cease to drift and tumble across the ground before them. Even Stanley stands frozen, his hands inches from the vortex.

"You're either the bravest human I've seen since I got here or the most foolish," the voice booms. "It looks like I finally found it, something not of this world," it continues.

"This mass... Feels like it wants my words. This has to be his... Lexicon's."

"This feeling... like freedom itself. That must be it. Time said the next time we met it'd have to be with *liberty*." The voice says, speaking towards the rift.

"You're in there, aren't you?" the voice asks but no reply comes from the rift. There is a certain feeling it exudes, however, like the limitless expanse of freedom, locked behind a cage. A feeling Prevention can't describe any more than that and hopes she'll never have to again after today.

"Escape..." she reads with a nod of her head, now standing besides Stanley. "That doesn't sound like something Lexicon would want for you, so, I guess it's up to me to do it then," the embodiment says as she reaches for the rift.

The rift darts backwards as if reflexively, and hovers back into the air, far above any natural height.

"You went still for the human, but not for me. You must not like the prospect of an embodiment going in there," Prevention says to the rift. "That has to mean Freedom's really there."

The rift begins to fly away. Watching it go, the embodiment stretches out her palm and utters the word "Stop."

The rift freezes in place.

"You're fighting this, I can tell. I'll have to work fast," she says. "But first, I've got to make sure no humans get involved in this."

At once the embodiment outstretches her arms and releases a pulsing wave that expands to a mile-wide perimeter.

"That'll prevent any of you from seeing this thing," she says, much to herself. "You'd all just get in my way."

The embodiment prevents the effect of gravity upon herself as she leaps towards the rift. Prevention soars through the air as her weightless body carries her towards the gyre.

"I'm getting you out of there, Freedom," Prevention shouts as she makes contact.

She is instantly swallowed by it and vanishes from sight.

Stanley unfreezes. He's confused. He could've sworn he was just... He looks up. There's nothing to see other than a heavyset black sky with a few stars beginning to poke their way through.

He stands in the middle of the street for a few moments before accepting the fact that he must be seeing things. Perhaps a concussion from the blows earlier or mere exhaustion, he concludes.

Stanley looks down at his hands. There is a paper bag full of food in one and a drawing of a candle in the other. *Get home,* he thinks. After arriving at the house he knocks on the door and is greeted by a pair of eager eyes through the peephole. It's a certain lapsing vegetarian. Stanley smiles back and enters safely, both resources and mental state in hand. It's going to be a good night, he thinks to himself as the door closes and locks swiftly behind him.

For Prevention, however, the tribulations have only just begun.

PREVENTION IS EJECTED from the other side of the rift, landing with a barrel-roll which breaks her fall out of the gateway's mouth. She stands up to unfamiliar surroundings. Everywhere she looks, words and letters comprise everything around her. Words and letters constituting the sky above her like a blanket floating over the landscape. Words and letters bundled together in various shapes hovering in the air like clouds. She looks down. Words and letters even making up the land she stands on, the word ground repeated indefinitely for as long as the land stretches.

"Lexicon's domain," Prevention says. "I made it."

As Prevention speaks, the words she just spoke appear physically in front of her, as if spawning from nothingness.

"When I speak..." she starts, and those words appear in front of her, too.

Prevention waits for a moment as the words she has spoken surround her. A few seconds later, the words encompassing her break up into their constituent letters and the letters scatter through the domain until Prevention can no longer see them.

"Hmm," Prevention hums. Even that minor vocalization is converted into a word.

Hmm floats in front of her before the letters disperse into the otherwise stagnant abyss. The 'H' aimlessly soars around until it is out of Preventions's sight, while the m's shoot off towards a mountain of words in the distance.

Prevention watches the m's leave, before she says the word "Mountain."

The word appears in front of her before separating into its constituent letters. The symbols quickly shift back into the word they originated, *mountain,* soaring back toward the mountain of words.

"This place uses letters to complete the words that make up this domain." Prevention amuses, slightly impressed.

"Now... if the word mountain gravitated toward the mountain and if the word sky gravitates to the sky, then how about... Prevention"

Prevention ignores all of the words appearing in front of her as they spring forth and disperse, all except for the word *prevention*, which she watches intently. The word 'mountain' shoots towards the nearest mountain, the word 'sky' shoots towards the sky, yet *prevention* rises into the air wanting to break apart and disperse, instead glitching almost in a display of confusion, and soars straight to Prevention and attaches to her arm like a tattoo. There isn't anything in existence that epitomizes the word *prevention* more than Prevention herself. Not even in Lexicon's domain.

Now Prevention knows her task.

"Freedom," she says.

She stands and watches the word rise into the air, glitch, then soar in the direction of one of the mountains in the distance.

Prevention smirks, "So that's where you are."

Before the term can veer too far ahead of her, she

outstretches a hand and exerts her expression on the word, stopping it mid-air so she can walk closer to it before letting it continue to lead. She follows the word freely this way as it travels through Lexicon's domain.

As they move toward the intended destination, Prevention bears witness to all manners of word-configurations possible throughout the domain. Trees comprised of the word *tree*, rivers of flowing words loosely scripted with their aquatic namesake– even a radiating "Light" encompassing much of the sky with a luminous glow commandeering authority over the domain.

After about forty minutes Prevention is still following the soaring word deep into the domain, now deep into a valley, ensuring she never gets too far away from the word as it travels. Suddenly, she hears a high-pitched screech coming through the air. Prevention looks up to see a winged creature in the shape of a bird, composed entirely of the word *sentry* flying high above. The creature screeches again, this time looking down while flying, and the word 'echo' repeatedly leaves its mouth in a cone as it screeches. Prevention watches as one of the words 'echo' bounces off of the word 'Freedom' in front of her and returns to the sentry bird, the bird swooping down towards where the echo bounced off from.

Prevention realizes the bird is engaging in a sweep of the area, trained to look for anything out of place in the domain. She spots a tree not far from her and sprints towards it, leaving the word she's following suspended mid-air in the middle of the valley. Prevention climbs the trunk and nestles herself between lush green repetitions of the word *leaves* within the tree's crown. Meanwhile, the sentry scouts out the perimeter by emitting monotonous screeches. Successfully, an echo bounces against her hiding spot but the bird ignores the signal it receives back, noting only the tree, and not the embodiment. Once the Sentry feels its directive complete, it returns to the pursuit of tracing the sovereign word.

The bird snatches the word and begins to fly away, but not before a speeding branch hurls toward it and knocks the winged creature from flight.

Prevention walks over to the immobile bird.

"Sorry, but I still need this," she says as she pries the word from the sentry's mouth. She frees the word and allows it to continue on its original path.

She bends down and puts her hand to the sentry bird's chest. She feels its life has not stopped, or rather been prevented from continuing.

"Good. You'll live."

As Prevention follows along, it begins to rain, the words mirroring the act of pouring droplets. Once hitting the earth, the words transforming to *wet* and so on and so forth, everything coming into contact with another element exhibiting a game of wordplay.

On her next step, Prevention is taken by surprise as her foot begins to sink into the ground. Looking down, she sees that the words 'wet-ground' have changed into 'mud' as more 'rain' pours. Before Prevention's leg is enveloped further than her knee, she uses her expression to prevent the rain within a 10 meter vicinity of herself from bonding with the 'ground'; preventing any more 'wet-ground' from forming, and thus preventing any further 'mud' from being created. Prevention then stops the suction affecting her enveloped leg, pulling her leg out of the already created 'mud'.

In her occupation with her sinking leg and prevention of the mud from forming, Prevention realizes she has lost sight of the word 'Freedom' as the rain obscures her view of the surroundings. Not accepting the defeat, she outstretches her arms to either side of herself, and within moments all activity within a half-mile radius stops. This creates a half-a-mile wide dome of stasis around Prevention, where the falling words of rain are simply suspended in the air. Falling rain outside of the half-mile radius that lands within the field of the dome is stopped dead in its tracks when it enters the half-mile radius, giving the dome a shell of suspended 'raindrops'. Somewhere within the dome, Prevention knows, floats the stopped word 'Freedom'.

Prevention remembers that the word was traveling towards the mountain in the distance when she was last following it. Taking that as her starting point, she begins to walk through the suspended 'raindrops' in the direction of the word mountain, parting the rain like a curtain as she walks through it. Finding it difficult to parse through the monumental amount of rain to find one single word, Prevention allows everything within the half-a-mile dome but the word 'Freedom' to resume activity, which results in all of the suspended rain falling to the ground. She maintains her expression's effect, preventing the 'rain' from bonding with the words that make up the ground, though. Sure enough, Prevention identifies the word 'Freedom' floating in the air. Satisfied, she then turns her head to the sky, and with a slightly strained grunt and furrow of her eyebrows, prevents the typographic clouds from releasing raindrops entirely for as far as the domain stretches. Having thus neutralized the rain, she continues following the word 'Freedom', through the domain.

Eventually, she reaches the other side of the valley, and begins to climb her way out, getting closer to the word-mountain with every passing step. When she crosses the highest point of the valley, she begins walking in the direction of the mountain straight ahead of her roughly a kilometer away. The closer she gets to the mountain, the more she notices the small creatures comprised of words scurrying around the area. She squints and scrutinizes one. It is made up of the word 'bug'. Another made up of the word 'mouse'.

"This world... It's as if it contains every word one could imagine. Is this where Lexicon came from?"

Expecting her words to simply disperse into the environment like before, Prevention is surprised when she sees the words begin swirling in a tornado, shooting off towards the same mountain the word 'Freedom' has been traveling towards.

"What has Lexicon got going on up there? What're they doing to you?" She says, looking at the word as it travels.

Soon, Prevention faces the base of the mountain. As she had surmised, it consists entirely of the word *mountain* as far up as she can see. The word 'Freedom' floats upwards towards the peak of the mountain. Prevention follows the word on foot for as long as she can as it rises, until parts of the mountain become too steep for her to simply walk. Instead of climbing rock-face to rock-face, Prevention prevents the effect of gravity the domain has acting on her body, allowing her to leap up the side of the mountain, subsequently grabbing a hold of the next piece of the mountainside as she elevates, following the word 'Freedom' up.

After twenty minutes of launching herself up the side of the mountain, Prevention finally reaches the top of the mountain. Climbing over the ledge of the mountain-top, she stands up to face the entity she has come all this way to see, across from her on the flat peak of the mountain, chained by his neck, arms and legs to the summit of the mountain by the words *bind* and trapped inside of a cage of made up of the word *constrict*, a tornado of swirling letters above his head. The word Freedom soars towards the constricted man through the bars of the cage and attaches itself to his arm like a tattoo.

"Freedom," Prevention says. "I've finally found you."

Freedom looks back at her and says, "Seems like I've become quite popular. Are you here to finish what Lexicon started?"

"I'm here to get you out of this place."

"You risked coming here for me?"

"Freedom ought to be defended when it's in jeopardy. I'm just doing my job to prevent the threat that was posed when you were taken from being realized."

"Your job.... Just who are you?"

"The name's Prevention."

Prevention strolls towards the caged Freedom. As she gets closer, the tornado of letters swirling above Freedom's head separates and the letters accumulate on the floor between the two embodiments. Both whirlwinds coagulate into large bodies finalized in one familiar word: *golem.* The apparitions form holding a mass of letters that represent a large broadsword and warhammer respectively.

"It doesn't look like this is going to go peacefully," Freedom laments as the golems stand ahead and block his path.

The threats begin to advance, raising their weapons.

"This doesn't have to *go* at all," Prevention says, stretching out her palm toward the two.

The golems stop in their tracks.

"You... You froze them," Freedom says.

"I prevented them from moving."

"Like your namesake... I could tell you're an embodiment. But something about you feels... out of place?"

"Out of time. I shouldn't have emerged in this era yet, but you could say I was sent here on a mission. Now, let's get you out of there."

Prevention walks between the two frozen golems until she is standing face to face with Freedom.

"This era? A mission from who?" Freedom questions.

"You'll meet him soon enough. He's the kind who'd probably prefer it best if I kept his name out of the limelight before you two are introduced."

"Fine. I just hope he makes for a better conversationalist than Lexicon."

"You two spoke?" Prevention asks, touching the cage.

"Not long enough."

"Was his plan all along to take you?"

"I don't think so. He said he'd only intended to take the word *free* from existence. Unbeknownst to him was that you can't just constrict the word without constricting me too. I am that which is only free. I am freedom itself. I can't be free if my name isn't, call it an unforeseen vulnerability. Either all of me is free, or none of me is. When Lexicon took the word away I ended up here, chained and caged to this domain. Lexicon told me he didn't like that I had to be constricted along with the word, but all the same, he told me if that's what needed to happen then it was a cost he was willing to pay."

"He might be the embodiment of words, but when his machinations begin to affect other embodiments, he crosses a line that involves me."

Prevention punches one of the bars of the cage and it doesn't so much as budge.

"Damn. Feels unbreakable. Unless I could use... Prevention starts.

"Watch out!" Freedom shouts as a warhammer connects with Prevention's side and thrusts her as far as the distant mountain-top edge.

"Urgh," Prevention groans, rolling herself back to her feet and sliding to a stop before falling off the ledge. She looks up to see the warhammer-wielding golem approaching, while the sword-wielding golem begins to twitch with movement.

"I thought you stopped them!" Freedom yells.

A stream of blood runs down one of Prevention's nostrils.

"Holding back all of the rain in this domain must've taken more out of me than I thought." she admits, as she readies herself into a combat stance, fists clenched in front of herself.

The sword-wielding golem begins moving fluidly and both approach Prevention.

"I'll have to do this the old-fashioned way then," Prevention mutters, before sprinting toward both golems.

Prevention reaches the sword-wielding golem first. It brings its sword down which Prevention evades by darting to the left side of the golem. Before the golem can turn to face her, Prevention jumps onto the golem's back and delivers a maelstrom of blows to its head. Prevention launches herself off of the golem's back, returning to the ground and performing a leg sweep on the creature, tripping it to the ground.

Still splayed, her eyes fix on the warhammer-wielding golem bringing down its hammer on her. Prevention's eyes widen, but don't close. Instead, the golem staggers, prevented from moving for just a moment long enough for Prevention to roll to the side of the cratering impact. By this time, the sword-wielding golem has begun to stand itself back up, using the sword as a pole to support its weight as it stands, and Prevention is surprised to see the golem uninjured from all of the blows she landed to its head.

Standing up, with a second stream of blood now running down her other nostril, Prevention says "These golems are as tough as the cage bars. These are some strong words."

"If you can't win just run! I don't need your blood on my hands!" Freedom shouts from behind his cage.

"You don't need to worry about me, Freedom. I had a plan for getting you out of there. I guess I'll just need to use it on the golems too."

And with that Prevention vanishes from sight.

The golems turn their heads from side to side, scanning the mountain summit for any sign of the embodiment, finding none. Suddenly, the sword is ripped from the golem's hand and plunges deep into its stomach. The sword cuts upward through the golem from its own stomach, slicing it from torso to skull. Once its head is peeled in two the golem drops to the ground and disperses into a pile of despondent letters.

Prevention reappears sword in hand, and before the war hammer-wielding golem can react, Prevention throws her weapon like a javelin through her opponents forehead, who similarly sinks into the ground and disseminates into a pile of letters.

"You can go invisible?" Freedom asks, unable to hide his impressed tone.

"I can prevent myself from being seen. I might be grid-locked for now though," Prevention says, setting the sword against the cage. "Now, let's get you out of there."

"These words might be tough, but when used against each other..." Prevention continues, lifting the warhammer up and swinging against the bars of Freedom's cage. They shatter into their constituent letters and fall to the ground, creating an opening in the cage. After two more swings the cage is opened wide enough on one of its sides for Prevention to enter inside of it. Putting down the warhammer and picking the sword back up, Prevention steps inside the cage raising the sword high above herself.

"Don't move," She warns.

"I couldn't if I tried," Freedom says.

Prevention brings the sword down hard against the

chains enclosing Freedom's arms and legs, cutting Freedom loose of his bondages. Prevention then places the sword against the chain against Freedom's neck, and pulls back the sword, readying herself to swing.

"You better not have gone through all of this work just to decapitate me," Freedom says.

"Relax," Prevention replies as she swings the sword at Freedom's neck and cuts through the iron restraints just enough to set him free– never once allowing the blade to so much as graze his tender skin.

"I know when to stop," Prevention says, with a novel grin.

"Yes...Ok. Is humor one of your expressions, too?" Freedom asks facetiously as he rubs wrists which for him feel like they've been bound for eternity.

"There's nothing wrong with lightening the mood every once in a while," Prevention says.

"On that we can agree," Freedom admits. "Before the revelry though, we should probably get ourselves out of here."

"There was a rift I came through to get here. If we can reach it, that's our way out," Prevention agrees as they side-step the broken chains and head toward the summit.

"Now that I'm free, If you give me a couple of minutes, I can–" Freedom starts, interrupted by a fist to the temple that throws him to the ground. Prevention turns just in time to see another golem coming into existence, from the same swirling tornado of letters above the cage of letters.

"Freedom!" Prevention shouts, performing a jump kick that knocks the golem back. She grabs Freedom's hand and picks him up from the ground.

"We've got to get out of here, now!" she says as both embodiments run to the cliff of the mountain.

Freedom turns around to see two more golems being built from the word tornado.

"There's nowhere to go!" Freedom shouts back.

"There is! Down!" Prevention says, grabbing Freedom by the hand.

"Damnit– I hope we survive this." And they jump.

Hand in hand, Freedom and Prevention glide through the air down the mountain as they fall towards the ground. Prevention is silent as she falls but Freedom lets his voice be heard.

"AAAAAHHH!"

1000 meters to the ground.

Prevention looks at Freedom.

800 meters.

Freedom looks back at Prevention.

500 meters.

Prevention clutches Freedom.

300 meters, the ground is getting close.

Freedom closes his eyes.

200 meters.

Prevention outstretches her free hand towards the ground.

100 meters– they are going to crash.

50 meters.

They begin to slow down mid-air.

30 meters, their fall becomes a slow hover.

10 meters. They *stop* mid-air.

Freedom opens his eyes as the two land safely onto the ground.

Freedom gets up first. "We made it! How did we-?" He looks to his side to see Prevention panting on the ground.

"I thought you said you were gridlocked."

"I thought I was... but I guess having our lives in peril... gave me an extra push," Prevention replies between huffs.

"Now we just need to get to that rift. And fast," she continues as she stands to her feet.

"It's like I was saying at the top of the mountain, if you give me a few minutes we can-"

Just then, a sound like the flapping of wings is heard approaching Prevention and Freedom. Both look up to see two winged golems soaring towards them from the mountaintop.

"Run!" Prevention shouts as both she and Freedom begin sprinting through the domain.

"We don't need the rift! I can free us from this domain's entrapment!" Freedom shouts mid-sprint.

"What stopped you from doing that all this time?" Prevention shouts back to him.

"I was constricted. Now that I'm out of that bondage, I'm reacclimating to my concept."

"I don't follow!" Prevention says, as she turns her head back to see the flying golems coming within problematic distance of the two embodiments.

"Freedom is to be unrestricted. In other words, at standard performance I'm not restricted by anything, including location. That means I'm free to choose where I want to be!"

"Can you turn those minutes it'll take to get us out of here into seconds?" Prevention asks as she sprints beside Freedom.

"That depends on where we need to go."

The golems are closer than 100 meters now.

"Escape has already been made with the rift," Prevention tells him.

"Yes, I can feel the exit from here. It is freedom from this place."

"Then what's stopping us?" Prevention says

"Take my hand and find out!"

The golems are right behind the two of them. One raises its arm, preparing to strike the embodiments just as Prevention grabs Freedom's hand. The golem brings down its arm as Prevention and Freedom vanish, leaving the golems alone, their directive failed.

A second later, Prevention and Freedom fall to the ground with the swirling rift above them. It is night time. They are in a park.

"We made it back," Prevention says.

"This place... Where are we?" Freedom questions.

"Welcome to Earth. This is where Lexicon's taking of words started."

"Then this is where he took the word 'free' away from first. That explains the feeling I'm getting. All around me, I can feel the lack of freedom. The inhabitants of this world's inability to use words."

"But now that you're free..."

"Yes, they should be too," Freedom says, closing his eyes. He grits his teeth, and a moment later, opens his eyes.

"I've freed them. Every word-speaker on this planet. At the least they should be able to use the word 'free' again. Just as it took time for me to acclimate to freedom however, it may take some time before these word-speakers-"

"Humans," Prevention interjects.

"... It may take some time before these humans regain their freedom to use any words."

"How long might that be?" Prevention asks.

"With Lexicon still on the loose restricting word usage, much longer than one would want. The humans will be able to use the word freely for as long as I am free, but the other words are part of Lexicon's jurisdiction, not mine, so my attempting to free them of all of Lexicon's restrictions is an uphill battle."

"Then he still needs to be stopped," Prevention says.

"Yeah," Freedom agrees.

"You can leave that to me," Prevention says. "Right now though, I think it's about time you met your benefactor."

"You did say something about being sent on a mission by someone, didn't you?"

"Yeah. Hold on." Prevention initiates the *timeout* sign with both of her hands. "This is a little trick he taught me to call him. He should be here in Three.... Two...-"

"You're getting better at *almost* stopping time there, Prevention. At least within your immediate vicinity," a voice calls out.

Freedom turns around to see a tall figure standing behind him.

"It's like trying to keep a drop of water from traveling with the rest of the stream. *Almost* might send you a signal, but it isn't close enough to actually do anything more than call you," Prevention replies.

"That's still far better than anyone else I've ever met, P."

"Well you've trained me well, Time."

Freedom's eyes widen.

"You're... Time?"

"As much as clocks tell it. You're Freedom, I presume?" Time replies.

"Yes." Freedom nods.

"Well done on your mission, Prevention. Freedom, we have much to discuss. I have questions for you I mean to ask."

Freedom looks at both embodiments for a moment, and turns to Time.

"Alright. What do you want to kn-" he starts.

"Away from here. Lexicon will be here soon," Time interjects.

Freedom tilts his head- "You can tell?"

"The flow of time, while linear for you, is more like a book to me. A book which I can open to any page. I can see everything that has and might still transpire here. Lexicon's arrival is one of those events. A highly likely event, even given the fickle nature of the future," Time replies.

"You can leave him to me. I'm going to stick around here until Lexicon shows up. Someone needs to stop him," Preventions says.

"A valiant decision. I'm glad I sent you on this mission. I take it this means you don't want me to send you back to your era?"

"Not until the job is done."

"Very well. Come then, Freedom. Let's get going. We can't waste the opportunity Prevention is giving us." Time says, as he begins to walk away from the spot under the rift.

Freedom follows, and soon, both are out of sight of Prevention.

"Did you know Prevention was going to choose to stay?" Freedom asks.

"Some events are more likely to happen than others. Lexicon arriving at the rift is a nearly fixed moment in time in its likeliness. Prevention choosing to stay wasn't."

"So you saw an outcome where Prevention didn't decide to stay?"

"I can see all branching timelines."

"How do you live with that kind of burden?"

"It's all I've ever known," Time says, turning to look at him.

"Can you choose which timeline happens?"

Time doesn't answer.

"That's what you did when you sent her back to save me, isn't it?"

"I intervene when it is necessary, not to bring about a certain timeline, but to prevent ones from happening that shouldn't be."

"And Lexicon taking words was one of those timelines?"

"Yes."

"Who gave you the right to decide that?"

"When you're the only one who can see how bad threats to existence are in the long run and have the capacity to avert them, wouldn't you? I am the embodiment of time, after all, so who else could safeguard it?"

Freedom is silent as he ponders the question.

"I don't meddle with timelines any more than when it comes to preventing bad ones, I can assure you. Anything else should be the untampered flow of time."

"Fine," Freedom says.

"I only want what's best for existence," Time says.

"So what would've happened if Prevention hadn't decided to stay?" Freedom questions.

"Nothing good. Especially not as good as this conversation."

"And you would've let that happen?"

"Getting Prevention to rescue you was the extent of my meddling. From here I was comfortable letting time play out."

"Okay, I trust you," Freedom says.

"My sending of Prevention to rescue you wasn't enough for that?" Time asks.

"I couldn't be certain. I am now."

"Good. Do you feel safe at this distance from the rift?" Time asks Freedom.

"We could always be safer. I'm free to be wherever I want to. How about I take you somewhere I know we can't be tracked?"

"That sounds acceptable to me," Time replies.

"Alright, brace yourself." Freedom says, as he puts his hand on Time's shoulder.

Both embodiments vanish from the face of the Earth and reappear in a region between Somewhere and Nowhere, debris floating around aimlessly.

"I call this region Elsewhere. There came a point where I wanted to be free of all locations, but at the same time, free from not being anywhere at all. I was testing the limits of freedom and this is where that test brought me. There are parts of this region even I struggle to get to, and I'm free to be anywhere I choose. Nobody could follow us here. We're safe."

"I'm impressed, Freedom. But just for good measure, I can pause time for us so we can hold this conversation interrupted. "

"Wait. I have a better idea. Have you ever made time?"

"It should be within my capacity. Why?" Time asks.

"I can give freedom to whatever I want. If you could make time, I could give it freedom to exist separately from the rest of time. Together we could make free-time." Free answers.

"I think I understand. It would be as if time were passing normally for everything around us –"

" – but we'd have a free moment of time to talk within for as long as we wanted," Freedom interjects.

"A moment only experienced by us through the interaction of our expressions," Time concludes.

"Exactly. You want to give it a go?" Freedom says, extending his hand for a handshake.

"Let's do it," Time says, taking his hand.

A bubble forms around both embodiments, extending from their shaking hands until it surrounds them both, and just like that, free-time has been made. Time passes normally on the outside of the bubble, but within it Freedom and Time engage in an entire conversation. The bubble pops a moment after it fully surrounds the pair. And in the span of that moment, Free and Time have finished their entire conversation. It went as follows:

"So that's how Lexicon trapped you..."

"Can he trap you again?" Time asks

"I haven't been trapped in decades before now. Lexicon caught me off guard when he took my name away, but now that I've experienced that kind of constriction, I know how to free myself of it. I've always managed to free myself before, but I wasn't prepared for that kind of entrapment. I am now. It'll be much harder for anything to attempt to constrict me again."

"Good. Then freedom is safe in your hands once again."

"Yes, and I'll ensure it stays that way."

"What do you intend to do, now that you're free?"

"All across existence, I can feel where Lexicon has taken my name. I'm going to go to each of those places and free them of at least that constriction, so they can continue to use the word. And I'll be doing my best to free them from the rest of his justice."

"Rescuing you was the correct course of action. I must ask though, how do you feel about Lexicon's taking of words beyond just the one that influences you?"

"As much as I hate seeing the perspective of my captor, I get it. Above every other motive, Lexicon is doing this because he despises hatred. Words are his domain, and so in a way he probably feels responsible for allowing hate speech to exist within a world he could take it away from."

"I understand. How do you feel about the conundrum he faces then?"

"If I were any other embodiment I might let him carry out his machinations without interruption, so long as it didn't come to affect me. But I'm not any other embodiment. I'm freedom itself. And above all else, it is my duty to uphold that freedom anywhere and everywhere I can. Hate speech is a vile plague that poisons every world it finds itself emerging from, but the solution being a world where hate speech isn't allowed to exist is a world where free-speech doesn't, and I can't help but oppose that."

"Are you saying you value free-speech over banning hate-speech?"

"I do. That's not to say I don't think hate-speech shouldn't beget consequences, just that a world where anyone isn't allowed to say what they really think is a far bleaker place than one where someone may introduce hatred into the world through the words they say."

"You'd be ok with a world full of hate if it meant that world had freedom?"

"I would. And I'd happily watch as that society crumbled under its own fault. The beauty of freedom is that it allows limitless opportunity. I see far more potential in any free world than a restricted one."

"I assume you're aware of laws? Conceptually, they restrict freedoms in the simplest sense. What of those?"

"If someone willingly gives up their freedoms without duress then who am I to judge?"

"I think I understand. I have my own reasons for stopping Lexicon, but your unique perspective on this entire calamity, given your position, is more meaningful to me than you know. I'll ponder on what you've said here for eras to come. Thank you, Freedom."

"I don't need thanks for my honest opinion, but I appreciate your consideration."

"Good. I suppose this brings me to my last question: What will you do if you encounter Lexicon again?"

"I'm free to be wherever I want, he won't be able to catch me."

"That does put me to ease."

"What will you do, Time?"

"I'll wait and see how things progress from here.

"You don't know how they will already?"

"There are still many ways this could play out. I'll let time run its own course."

"Okay."

"That is all, Freedom. I think we can end our free-time now.

And with that Freedom stretches his arm out in a fist-bump, and Time returns the gesture, amused.

The bubble pops.

"Do you want me to take you back to Earth now?" Freedom asks.

"No. I think I'll observe from here for the time being."

"Suit yourself. It is an interesting region."

"Perhaps I'll do some exploring then."

"Sounds good to me. I'll be off then, Time. I have places to free."

"Yes, you do. Good luck, Freedom."

"Will we see each other again?" Freedom asks, giving Time a final look.

"Only time will tell." Time says, smiling.

"Goodbye," Freedom says.

"Goodbye," Time replies.

Freedom vanishes, off to liberate countless worlds from Lexicon's grasp, leaving Time standing in Elsewhere, alone and in silence.

Time sits down and pulls out a notebook and a pen. Flipping through the empty pages, he says : "I think I'll call this *The Lexicon Saga*."

PART 2
2ND REPRIEVE

IN A MEDITATIVE POSITION with her legs crossed, Prevention sits atop the grass of the park eyes closed, Lexicon's rift swirling above her. Around Prevention bees buzz with the wind and birds chirp while soaring through the air, finding trees to perch themselves on. Nearby, squirrels scurry across the lush greenery as the sun rises and bathes nature in its soft, morning glow.

And while the fauna wake from their slumber to begin the day, Prevention remains immobile, as she sits on the serrated grass, with not even so much as the expansion and contraction of her breathing visible. More still, not even the blowing wind disturbs so much as a hair on her head. Prevention remains static in place, like a living statue, all motion, movement and activity *preserved*. She looks peaceful, as if enjoying the utter stillness of the moment. A moment of pause soon to be interrupted.

"What the hell?" a voice calls out.

For a moment, Prevention remains inanimate before slowly opening her eyes to face the source of the sound.

"Well, hello there," Prevention says as she stands up.

"You can talk? Who are you, and what are you doing

under that rift?" the source says, finally coming into view.

"I haven't had my words taken yet, but, I did prevent anyone from being able to see this," she says, referring to the rift. "How did you know it was here?"

"I'd know where one of my rifts were any day of the year. If you still have your words, you aren't any regular inhabitant of this world. You still haven't answered me– who are you?"

"Your rift... So you've finally arrived. I've been expecting you, Lexicon. You look wearier than I thought you'd be."

"You ignore my questions and now you say my name. I've had enough of that being called by strangers. I'd recommend telling me who you are, *now*," Lexicon says.

"I imagined you might be aggressive with the reputation you've made for yourself. Looks like I was right. I'm not here to fight if I don't have to. Let's just say I want to talk."

"I don't have time for this. Move aside. I have business to attend to," Lexicon says as he walks towards the rift, which has floated down to ground level.

Just as he gets within a few steps of the portal, Prevention places her hand on Lexicon's chest and blocks his entrance to it.

"If you're going to go looking for Freedom, don't bother. He's long gone by now."

Lexicon looks at Prevention, his eyes widening then eyebrows furrowing at the mention of Freedom.

"What did you just say?" Lexicon asks, his fist clenching. The rift swirls to a close before dissipating completely.

"You heard me. I didn't like what you did with him, so I gave him a hand."

"First you use my words. *My words.* Next, you fail to reveal your identity to me. And now, you tell me you've interfered with what should have never involved you. Are you sure you want to antagonize me?" Lexicon asks.

"From one embodiment to another, you antagonized yourself when you decided to take words away from existence. I'm just the one who's here to make sure you don't do any more harm than you've already caused," Prevention replies, removing her hand from Lexicon's chest.

"That explains why you can talk. Be thankful that I haven't taken words from our race as yet, though my inclination to grows with every passing encounter I have with one of our own. You aren't the first to tell me you want to prevent me from doing my work. Yet here I stand, words still in my palm. What do you think you could do?" Lexicon challenges.

"As we speak, people all around us will soon have their ability to express *freedom* again. I'd say that's a good start. You'd be wise to heed *my words* when I say there is more where that came from. Before that though, I want to understand why you're doing what you have. So explain it to me, Lexicon, why insist on taking words away from everyone around you?"

"It's simple. Words are my responsibility and I've deemed them safer away from the hands of the masses who choose to abuse them."

"You think humanity's abusing words?"

"I've lived around them long enough to have witnessed it. In Nazi Germany, the would-be despots in control of the nation twisted words to fit their sick view of the world; they imposed those words upon the population and corrupted their people with each and every repetition of words they chose to commandeer. In the regime of Soviet Union, the dictators in power made use of slogans, trigger words, and language meant to infiltrate the minds of their people in order to perpetuate a political system; which, while promising to bring equality to the people, only succeeded in bringing famine and death," Lexicon offers.

"Even today, humanity's chosen leaders are too afraid to use the words to confirm the genocidal actions of nations all around their globe. Instead people use words of hate against each other on this planet. Words to insult, shame, and disgrace each other for differences as small as the color of their skin or which humans they choose to love. They cannot be trusted to bear the privilege of using words without tarnishing them, something I cannot idly stand by and watch happen for any longer as the embodiment, and sole protector, of words," he concludes fervently.

"I didn't know humans did such a thing. But does that justify your taking away words from all of them, let alone the rest of the word-users across existence?" Prevention asks.

"Humanity were the first to develop words, and if they fell to defiling them as they have, nothing stops any other race from following the same path. Words are safer in my hands alone."

"You understand that when the day comes that you take words away from embodiments, you'll be putting existence in danger?"

"Let me ask you this, Prevention. As an embodiment, do you have some kind of inclination, maybe even a purpose, that you feel is your duty to fulfill?"

"I prevent what needs to be prevented."

"And just as you do that, it is my duty to uphold the sanctity and quality of words. Existence is worthless if the words within it are not truly upheld. So I will do anything and everything within my capacity to ensure they are protected, even if that means that they should be taken from embodiments as well."

"That's where I have to draw the line, Lexicon. I prevent what I prevent so existence can function. Embodiments are a necessary cog in the scheme of things— our emergences ensure the continuation of concepts. I wouldn't be here without the word *prevention*. And I've since prevented my fair share of threats to existence, yet none have posed a threat to it like you. Since their creation words have become an essential part of existence," Prevention explains.

"You may be the embodiment of words, but each embodiment embodies their own specific concept. And that's something you could never replicate. You can't uphold existence alone, and neither can any of us embodiments who have already emerged. New embodiments will always be needed to continue the development of existence. I won't let you get in the way of that."

"Then it appears we have come to an impasse, just like the embodiment I encountered before you."

"You could find another-"

"Stop talking. For an embodiment named Prevention, you seem to be unable to stop yourself from prattling on. I refuse another option. I watched them. I gave humanity hundreds of years to show me that they could change. They failed. I won't wait until language is desecrated beyond saving. Leave me to my responsibilities."

"That would be ignoring my own."

"Prevention, I haven't even taken words from embodiments yet. You have no quarrel with me."

"But you did take Freedom, and you kept him caged in your domain despite knowing as much. I can't trust that you won't eventually turn your word-taking on the rest of us. Besides, taking words from all of the other word-users across existence is cruel enough to warrant someone intervening."

"Is this the hill you want to die on?"

"I made a promise I'd stop you."

"Then let's settle this now." Lexicon says, pushing Prevention back.

"So be it. I'm done resting anyway," Prevention replies as she steadies herself and raises her fists.

The word *pulse* appears on Lexicon's palm, which he brings up to face Prevention.

"What the-" Prevention starts, before she is blown back by a gust emanating from Lexicon's palm, thrusting Prevention into the base of a tree which outlines the open field surrounding them. The trunk snaps in two upon Prevention's impact, causing the top half to fall forward. She rolls out of the way of its path. Standing up she sees Lexicon, his index-fingers pointed.

"I learned one thing from humans."

Splayed across Lexicon's forearm, the word *bullets* appear. High-speed letters move at over five-hundred metres per second as they blast from Lexicon's fingertips. Watching letter after letter travel toward her, Prevention sways to one side and dodges the frenzy of characters. One grazes her shoulder, drawing blood. A new line of letters sputters towards their target but stops mid-air, along with the trickling stream of blood. Lexicon brings his fingers to his face, noticeably confused.

"Hmm?" he questions.

Lexicon doesn't have much time to wonder, with Prevention sprinting towards him. Now within ten meters, Prevention is close enough to make out another word etching itself across Lexicon's forehead... *burn*. Lexicon opens his mouth and out spews a torrent of flames directed at Prevention, who darts to the side as she runs to avoid the flame's path. Lexicon closes his mouth and allows the word *radiation* to inflame his chest.

"So that's what you're doing." Prevention whispers as she darts.

Lexicon glows green and charges toward his opponent, fists raised. Prevention catches the punch with her bare hand, the glow of Lexicon's fist gone.

"Not while I'm around," Prevention says, rocketing a

punch into Lexicon's gut and knocking him back, following up with a kick to Lexicon's chin.

"... I've been hit harder. I've never had someone prevent my expression from working, though. Let's see how long you can keep that up." Lexicon says through clenched teeth as he lunges towards Prevention, who prepares herself by bringing up her guards. Lexicon abandons his feint and performs a low-swiping kick that sweeps Prevention off of her feet and sends her toppling to her back. Lexicon seizes the moment and gets on top of his contender, raining down punches in a sick fury. Lexicon draws blood as a gash tears apart Prevention's lower lip; Lexicon clasps both of his hands together above his head and swings them down like an anvil toward Prevention's skull. Instinctively Prevention thrusts her hips upwards and throws Lexicon off of her body, giving herself the chance to stand back up. Lexicon rushes towards Prevention.

"STOP!" Prevention shouts, and Lexicon is frozen mid-rush.

Prevention begins to barrage Lexicon with an assortment of punches and kicks and ends with a swift uppercut to Lexicon's motionless jaw. A moment later, Lexicon resumes motion and as if every single one of the attacks were thrown at once Lexicon is blown back and a cut across the side of his cheek forms where Prevention finishes her assault.

"Stop this madness, before one of us ends up beyond recovery," Prevention warns Lexicon.

"You hit harder that time... I won't stop fighting for as long as there are words to defend. If you won't understand that, then it'd be better if you didn't have words at all," Lexicon says, as the word *blood* runs down the side of his cheek.

"You wouldn-" Prevention is unable to complete her sentence.

She tries to speak but no words come out of her mouth.

"You have only yourself to blame. If you would've just–" Lexicon begins.

"Oh, shut up!" Prevention shouts.

"How?..." Lexicon questions.

"I can prevent a lot more than you think."

"That makes you a liability," Lexicon says. "Perhaps more than any other embodiment I've encountered thus far. And that's exactly why I need to deal with you here and now."

"You can try."

Lexicon furrows his brow as in front of him, a rift begins to swirl. Lexicon pulls back his hand and plunges it deep into the rift. When he pulls it back out again, he is holding a sword composed of letters. The rift dissipates and he runs towards Prevention, sword primed to slay. Prevention lunges backwards avoiding the slash, and spots a rock lying on the ground of the open field. She picks it up and launches it toward her mission, who splits the rock in two with his weapon. Seizing the distraction, Prevention charges, delivering a series of deafening punches to Lexicon's left temple. She lands a front kick to the chest.

As Lexicon is thrust backward, however, he freezes mid-path, and Prevention darts around to his backside and throws a punch squared at the back of Lexicon's skull; The punch rocks Lexicon forward just as he resumes moving and the crunch of his skull reveals the true underdog in this fight, his sword dropping to the floor.

Prevention axe-kicks Lexicon's back, knocking him further forward. Picking up the sword, Prevention lodges it into the grass of the field as Lexicon turns to face her, the words *heal* and *recover* latticed under his hair.

"That was pretty good," Lexicon says.

"I'm not fighting to impress you," Prevention replies.

"I know," Lexicon says, as he begins to sprint towards

Prevention. Outstretching his hand, the word-sword splits into its constituent letters and flies towards Lexicon. The letters stop mid-air between Lexicon and Prevention– "You aren't getting that back so easily. Nothing from here out is going to be easy for you to swallow." Prevention says, as Lexicon finds himself stopped once again, though this time, he can talk.

"Release me Prevention!"

"This is the only way we'll be able to talk. Now you will hear what I have to say."

"Once I get out of this, you're finished."

"No Lexicon. You're finished. You refuse to be reasoned with, so I'm just going to pull this out at the root..."

"Prevention, don't do this."

Blood starts trickling down Prevention's nose.

"Hrrg. I already have."

ALL AROUND THE GLOBE AND THROUGHOUT EXISTENCE, WORDS return to the mouths of those who can speak them.

On Earth, the first word that emerges is *hungry*, from the mouth of a baby, just old enough to say what's on its mind without needing a prompt.

"What?" the baby's mother asks, surprised she's hearing from the mouth of her child.

"You just spoke!" the mother's partner exclaims. "We can speak!"

Across the planet conversations begin happening on the off-chance someone attempts to use a word. Within a single minute, hundreds of thousands of words are being spoken, a number exponentially increasing every moment.

"What have you done?!" Lexicon shouts.

"Finished it," Prevention says, falling to one knee.

"This is hard for you, isn't it?" Lexicon sneers.

"I can keep this up for as long as it takes," Prevention retorts, weakly.

Lexicon's eyes widen, and soon a smile comes across his face.

"It's taking all the focus you have to prevent me from taking everyone's words. Too much focus for you to prevent everything else I can do."

"What are you-"

The word *banish* writes itself under Lexicon's right eye.

Prevention's eyes widen.

"Sto-"

Prevention begins flickering in and out of view.

"I learnt this one after being pulled out of space. There are a lot of places outside of space and reality. Let's see how well you deal with the furthest one from words that I can send you."

And just like that Prevention is shunted off to a place outside of space.

Lexicon begins laughing.

"Her prevention is becoming less effective with every moment. Words are mine to take once again."

And so they are taken. The euphoria of having their words back is short-lived, as people begin to lose their speech once more.

Lexicon stands in the middle of the open field, a smirk across his face, as a rift opens in front of him.

"Onto business," Lexicon says as he walks through the rift, followed by the letters Prevention once suspended.

Prevention reappears on a ground of marble composition, a clear white sky above her. All around Prevention outcrop protrude from the ground, rising dozens of meters into the air. Each outcrop's exterior provides seamless entrance into celestial vistas, some beyond compare. Besides the outcrop, Prevention can't make out any other discernible objects or life anywhere she looks. She is utterly alone.

"Where am I?" Prevention asks. The words come out of her mouth much louder than she would've expected and reverberate through the landscape. *Where am I,* the words echo. It is within these loud echoes that Prevention realizes how quiet her surroundings are– She can't hear a single sound. Prevention's heartbeat becomes apparent to herself, thumping incessantly without pause. Even the beat of her heart produces a slight echo, a testament to just how noiseless this location is. Likewise, she finds herself unable to ignore the sound of her own breathing, even the blowing of air in and out of her nose, louder than anything in her surroundings. It seems as though Prevention is the only thing producing any sound in this environment and that unnerves her as she walks. Soon, the echoes she produces reap their consequences. All around Prevention, the foreign outcrop begin to quaver as sound bounces off of them, their inner vistas storming.

Prevention lowers her center of gravity as she crouches down to avoid falling, but the beat of her heart steadily increases, only generating more echoes. There is an explosion within the vista of a storming outcrop, which bursts through the outcrop's exterior throwing Prevention back towards another storming jut, which looks to be composed entirely of a yellow star's consistency. Preventing the starry environment from harming her arms, Prevention pushes her head out of the solar outcrop and falls to the ground, her hair completely incinerated but eyebrows intact, courtesy of her expression.

"That's going to take a while to grow back", Prevention says, feeling her head. The residual matter from the burst bathes her surroundings in a floating, luminescent light. A faint hum buzzes from the exotic material.

"That was a close call. I've got to rethink helping Time out so much out of the goodness of my heart," she retorts.

Just then, the ground ceases its trembling and the foreign outcrop stop quaking. Prevention notices her heartbeat and the subsequent echoes they produce growing quieter and quieter with each passing moment as a shadow casts over her. Looking up, she sees a silhouette standing atop of one of the outcrops, its appendage stretched out toward her. Prevention blinks and the silhouette is gone. Scanning the outcrop frantically, she notices that even the humming luminescent matter becomes more silent with every passing second. The vicinity returns to a chilling quiet, and a bead of sweat begins to run down Prevention's face as the eeriness of her strange surroundings sets in.

Suddenly, she feels a sensation on his shoulder and she screams, turning around to face a transparent, humanoid figure. Her scream is cut short as the sound emerging from her mouth vanishes. The figure simply stares at Prevention before placing its index finger on its lip.

"Who are you?! What do you-" again, Prevention's words are cut short as the sounds coming out of her mouth vanish.

The figure, neither discernibly male or female yet more-or-less humanoid all the same, holds its index finger at its lips and stares at Prevention expectantly.

Prevention, still one edge, continues her line of questioning.

"What are you doing to my voi-" she asks as an outcrop quavers beside him.

The humanoid figure presses its index finger to Prevention's lip. Its glassy texture is cold to the touch. Prevention is disarmed by the affable action and gently removes the figure's finger from her face.

"Are you trying to hush me?"

The figure nods its head and points towards one of the

foreign excrescence for Prevention to watch.

The words *hush me* echo through the outcrop as one by one they each quiver and quake. The severely quavering outcrop begins to storm with a massive quake when the figure then turns towards it and wags its finger, the echoes dissipating. As quiet returns to the vicinity, the outcrops stop storming and return to an equilibrium within their inner worlds.

Prevention's eyes widen.

"Is my voice-?" The outcrop begins quaking once more and the figure shoots Prevention a glare. It puts its finger to its lip once more. For a moment, Prevention does go quiet. The figure nods its head in approval at Prevention's silence and begins walking.

Prevention follows the figure on foot, as her footsteps continue to generate echoes and upset the celestial environment. The figure, taking note of this, turns around and gives Prevention an up-and-down glance. They continue on, and from that moment none of Prevention's movements or bodily functions produce sound or echoes. Perplexed, Prevention can't help but question the figure as to how they accomplished the feat.

"How did you do that? What did you do?" Prevention asks a second time, when the figure refuses to answer.

The figure simply watches Prevention's attempt to speak for a second time before it shakes its head in disapproval; it carries on walking.

"No sounds... Fine. Maybe this'll do it..." Prevention mouths to herself.

Prevention grabs the shoulder of the figure and closes her eyes. They both stop moving, and when Prevention opens them again, she finds the figure staring back at her.

"Did it work?"

The figure puts its finger to its lip instinctively, but then tilts its head in confusion. It didn't see her mouth move when she spoke.

Prevention smirks.

"You can talk to me now. Really. This won't make any sounds."

The figure frowns but watching Prevention speak without physical action prompts the figure to play along.

"How?" it asks, and its mouth doesn't so much as twitch while asking the question.

"I remembered what it felt like when Thought spoke to me telepathically, so I prevented all of our functions other than the mental for a moment to see if we'd be able to pick up on each other's thoughts. Looks like it worked! Don't worry about the headache. It passes"

"Thought?"

"An embodiment. That's what I am too, the name's Prevention."

"Embodiment? Me embodiment."

"What? Why couldn't I tell? Who are you?"

"*Silence.*"

Prevention's head cocks back in shock and forward in understanding.

"So that's why you've been shushing me?"

"I hush you because this place needs silence," the embodiment replies.

"Where are we, anyway?"

"Serenity."

"So that's where Lexicon sent me. A place as far from words as possible. You can't so much as speak here without the threat of those outcrops blowing up in your face."

"Who is Lexicon?"

"Another one of us. An embodiment a few centuries older than me, as old as words themselves. And a troubled embodiment, at that."

"Troubled?"

"He's the embodiment of words, and he's angry. He's taking words from existence as punishment to everyone he feels is doing them injustice."

"No words... That's good here. No words anywhere, less noise. Lexicon does not sound so bad."

"You really believe that?"

"In the beginning, there was the perfect harmony of *Silence*. Then, *Reality* awoke and brought discord. Now, only here the last fraction of absolute silence remains. Reality woke itself, yes, but it developed because nothing was there to disturb its growth. From the quiet, things arise. Here in the Serenity, *more* develops. I emerged to maintain the quiet so more can grow."

"Looks like you're used to communication now... Is that what those structures and this land within Serenity are? 'More'?" Prevention asks.

"Yes. And if this Lexicon takes words away from existence, Around gets quieter. Less noise means more quiet places where More can arise."

"You feel the more quiet that arises the better..."

"Yes. Serenity expands with every moment I increase the range of silence surrounding it. But I must remain here to maintain the quiet, so I cannot travel to other regions to spread it. Lexicon's taking of words does."

"Only, his taking of words is going to put existence in danger as he takes away the words embodiments need to emerge."

"He takes words away from embodiments?"

"He'd already trapped an embodiment and tried to take my words away. So yes, he's beginning to strip words away from even us."

"*Hmm*. Cruel."

"Exactly. Is allowing Lexicon to continue jeopardizing

existence worth adding a little more quiet to it in the short run?"

Silence's eyebrows furrow. Finally, Silence replies.

"No. Serenity will continue to expand here as I add more silence to it. More will grow. Lexicon taking words from existence is not worth the risk to all it poses, even if it does add more quiet."

"I'm glad you understand. That's why I need to stop him."

"How?"

"I don't know yet. Maybe..."

Her fist twitches.

"No," she says, shaking her head.

"Maybe..."

Prevention pauses for a moment in contemplation. Her eyes flash with inspiration.

"I couldn't speak just now when you made me silent. It wasn't like you took away my words, but I might as well have had them gone..."

"Yes. As I told you, silence is necessary here for More to develop."

"Could you teach me how to do that? How to take away sound?"

"How could you learn to mimic my expression?" Silence asks.

"I prevent things. It's what I do. But I've never tried to prevent sounds. If you helped me, I could learn to pull it off on at least one target."

"Lexicon?"

"Yeah. If he wants to take away words then perhaps I can prevent his audibility. Then he'll realize what it's like to live without something crucial to him."

"Sound is neither crucial nor necessary to me. Millions of beings live happily without the full experience of it,"

Silence says through mental communication, clearly insulted by the prospect that making or hearing noise is anything crucial to a satisfying existence.

"But you emerged to maintain the quiet, just like language is inherent to word-users. If someone tried to give you sound, you might feel the same way as those losing their ability to communicate. Stopping Lexicon's sound might be a lesson that one can't take what shouldn't be taken."

"He may learn to appreciate the silence as I do."

"I'm willing to give it a shot either way. There's not much else I could do that wouldn't leave me completely vulnerable to his expression. Will you help me? I'll be spreading silence to one more being in existence should you help me. The more silence the better, right?"

"It is not my place to interfere. And even as I value silence, you do not entice me through the suggestion of taking his away, as if that will please me. You are young, if you only follow Lexicon's existence for a few centuries, why not wait until you mature your expression enough so you can handle stopping him the way you first wanted to?"

"Because there won't be that much time to mature before everything has come undone. If you don't help, there might not even be a More to cultivate if Lexicon's taking of words destabilizes existence."

"I cannot ignore that risk. I'll help you."

"That's good enough for me. Teach me how to stop sounds."

"Very well, come," Silence says as it turns around and begins walking its original path. Prevention follows.

The pair arrive at what appears to be the edge of the land. In front of them exists only a white blankness. As Prevention looks down she can see the ground on the edge of land slowly extending. Like before, Prevention can't hear so much as a sound.

"More grows here. This is the boundary of Serenity," Silence tells Prevention while pointing at the blankness. "This is where you will learn."

"What would you have me do?" Prevention asks in reply.

"Extend Serenity by making more silence around it."

"That's what you said you do. You're having me do your job?"

"I didn't say I was helping you for free."

"... Fine. I'll do it. How do I start?"

"First, you must find the noise you wish to quiet."

"I don't hear a single thing here. How do you find noise through silence?"

"I am Silence. At all times I am aware of how far the quiet extends, and, if you want to make silence, you must know how to find the noise you wish to cancel."

"I can't just sense how far the vicinity of silence extends, but maybe I can tell where that vicinity *stops?*"

"Any method will do if it brings about the same result."

"Where the quiet stops... I've never had to *listen* for where something stops."

"Try."

Prevention closes her eyes in focus. She turns her head so her ear points towards the whiteness surrounding the edge of the land.

Listening to the silence more deeply than she ever has before, Prevention finds herself becoming lost in the noise-less tranquility that the quiet brings. For a moment she feels like she understands why Silence so vehemently maintains this peace. Then, as a spark might light up a dark room, she *hears* the noise barrier. She isn't used to it, but soon she becomes attuned to hearing where things *stop*.

"I hear it! Where the silence stops: noise. Surrounding the entirety of Serenity. It's otherworldly! It's like nothing I've ever heard in space before."

"Good. Now that you have found the noise, you must turn it to silence."

"How would I start? I've never successfully stopped anything as ambient as noise. It's everywhere. I don't know where to focus my expression."

"Think of noise as vibrations. When an object or particle vibrates, it causes the surrounding air molecules to vibrate, which results in a chain reaction of sound waves propagating through the environment. When I induce silence, I create a field which vibrations cannot propagate through, thus preventing sound waves from traveling through the field. More than that, I bring any noise I can hear to an equilibrium with its environment, until it reaches the perfect harmony or perfect disharmony of noise. Perhaps that may be above your means..."

"I'll stick to the first part. Vibrations huh... that makes things more tangible. Alright, I think I can try."

Prevention stretches her open hand out towards the blank whiteness and clenches it into a fist. At that moment, the vibrations surrounding Serenity begin erratically pausing and resuming vibration until they stop completely.

"The vicinity up until the noise is expanding," Prevention says, as she traces the area around her in search of where the quiet stops.

"Yes. I can feel the quiet extending. You were successful," Silence replies.

"The sound waves want to cause vibration. I can feel it. There are so many of them. I'm not sure how long I can keep them from propagating," Prevention says as her arm begins to tremble.

"Then train your prevention to last. If you want to maintain silence, you must be capable of sustaining it."

"How long do I have to keep this up until I can sustain

the silence?" Prevention asks, a bead of sweat running down her forehead.

"Until the only thing preventing silence is your choice not to induce it."

Prevention's arm shakes until she can no longer keep it up. When its falls back to her side, the vicinity of silence lessens back to where it was originally.

"Dammit! I don't have time for this. I need to stop Lexicon as soon as possible."

"Then you had best learn to wield silence soon. Come, again." Silence says, guiding Prevention to once again quell the noise surrounding them both.

"I'll get it right this time. I have to," Prevention says, raising her hand once again in attempts to prevent the vibrations.

<hr>

Two days have passed, as Prevention sits in a meditative pose, eyes closed, against the slowly extending edge of More. She opens her eyes and stands up. Silence is beside her.

"I'm ready," Prevention says

"Are you sure? You've only managed to maintain the silence you induced for a continuous ten hours."

"I have to be. I can't waste anymore time."

"Very well. What do you intend on doing now?"

"I have an embodiment to stop. I need to get back to him."

"How will you do that? Serenity is far removed from the space that you are from."

"I've been practicing more than just stopping noise here. I met an embodiment who was *free* to be wherever he wanted. It gave me an idea to *stop* being where I am. Or more accurately, to prevent myself from being somewhere."

"I see."

"Thanks for helping me, I hope our efforts will be enough."

"Your efforts. I only taught you to protect Serenity. Should Lexicon's taking of words fail to jeopardize existence and Serenity, I have no qualms with his actions. This is your battle to fight."

"It is. But I'll keep the vibrations surrounding Serenity stopped here. Call it a token of my appreciation."

"That will not be necessary. Your command over inducing silence is rudimentary at best. I'll continue expanding Serenity alone. You worry about your own mission."

"If that's what you wish."

"It is."

"Okay. Then this is where I leave you, Silence. Take care of yourself. Silence is tranquil, but it can be lonely."

"Company only brings noise. I prefer solitude. However, once you found a way for us to communicate without producing sounds, your presence was not... unpleasant."

"That almost sounds like you liked having me here. I won't forget that, Silence. Your speech showed major improvement as we kept talking telepathically. Let's see each other again one day. I'll be sure to keep quiet" Prevention says through her mind with a wink.

"I might like that."

"I might like that, too. See you around, Silence."

"Goodbye, Prevention."

And with that, Prevention is gone, leaving Silence alone in Serenity as More continues to develop under its feet. Celestial outcrops begin to protrude from the ground as Silence smiles and turns around, its duty to guard the land consuming its thoughts once more.

8 / SILENCE IS DEAFENING

PREVENTION REAPPEARS at the top of a mountain composed of words, a sky of words above her, and a ground made of words far below her. Sitting in the center of the summit an embodiment sits, his back facing Prevention, as he slams a hammer made of words into an anvil made of like substance. With each strike of his tool a clang rings distinctly and with it a letter rises into the air from the anvil, binding itself to the next letter which forms.

"Vinwedril," this particular word reads and Prevention doesn't understand what it means.

Next, the word *portal* etches itself across the back of the sitting embodiment, and an opening emerges beside the word *vinwedril*. Through the portal Prevention can see a vascular world of interconnected wheeling threads. The new word floats through the portal into the world of threads where it assimilates with the realm and the portal disperses.

"I just gave that place a word to describe it, that's the kind of thing I do," the embodiment says, turning his head towards Prevention.

Prevention takes a step back, shocked that her presence was detected.

"This is my domain. Don't be so surprised that I can tell what's in it." Lexicon says, turning around to face Prevention.

"Something about you has changed... New haircut?"

"Very funny." Prevention says.

"Though I would like to know how you managed to get here, let alone getting back into space?"

"I could only pull it off remembering what being near you was like." Prevention replies, having collected herself from his prior shock. The words she speaks appear in front of her before dispersing through the domain.

"Interesting. From the moment I gleaned your expression I knew you were a threat to me like no other embodiment, but I didn't expect you to come this far. Your words are unwelcome. That won't be happening anymore," Lexicon says, referring to the manifestation of spoken words within his domain.

"What do you intend to do now, prevent me? Prevent this? was it? You can't stop me from taking words without making yourself vulnerable to my expression. And believe me, now that I'm rested if you do so again I will do far worse than banish you;" Lexicon says, as a tornado of letters comes down from the sky and hovers behind him.

"I'm trying something different this time," Prevention says, as she takes a step forward towards Lexicon.

As soon as her foot touches the ground it is enveloped by the words making up that ground. With her foot partly submerged into the summit of the mountain, Prevention is unable to move freely.

"Everything in the wordscape responds to my will. You're fighting more than just me here," Lexicon tells his adversary as he raises his hand which causes a tornado of words to condense into a javelin floating above his hand. Lexicon thrusts his hand down as the javelin launches forward in a sonic boom.

Before the javelin hits Prevention it stops mid-air in front of her face. She reappears behind Lexicon with a thrown fist only to find herself suddenly sinking in a word-ridden ground. As she drifts downward a golem appears made entirely out of letters. The golem extends a hand which blocks Prevention's fist and uses the other to strike a blow itself. Prevention is dazed as she sinks lower into the soil.

Fully submerged to her chest, she turns to Lexicon.

"I'll make sure you never take another breath," he threatens, as the top layer of letters begin to revolve around her. Beneath the surface letters continue to tear at Prevention as they revolve in opposite directions all around her.

Prevention shouts in pain before the letters stop.

"You really do have a troublesome expression, Let's see how much it can really take," Lexicon retorts as the sky of words begin to descend toward them like a crushing blanket.

"Words could never harm me, but may this be the end for you" Lexicon says as the sky of words descend on their position.

"Not if I have anything to say about it," Prevention grunts. And just as suddenly, both embodiments reappear at the same park Lexicon once banished Prevention from.

Prevention reappears on her knees and only catches herself from falling face first into the grass at the last second. Lexicon reappears ten meters in the air above the park grass, falling to his feet gracefully in front of Prevention.

"Back here again?" Lexicon says, with stark annoyance in his voice.

"I want you to be near the people you hurt when I stop you," Prevention replies as she picks herself up from her knees.

"You haven't been doing a good job of that so far."

"I wasn't expecting you to be in that world of words when I stopped myself from being everywhere but where you were. Now that we're here though, it's fair game," Prevention tells him.

"You've only slightly delayed your final moment in bringing me here. Let's settle this."

"Yeah, let's."

Around Lexicon rifts open which letters outpour from. They condense into four new golems standing on the field, each with a weapon made of words in their hands. The golems and Lexicon begin charging at Prevention.

"Enough! I'm done fighting you, Lexicon!" she shouts.

The golems stop dead in their tracks as Lexicon follows suit.

"You've taken words from those who rely on them. So now, I'm going to prevent you from having something and see how you fare. I call this *muting*."

"What are you talking about?" Lexicon asks. Only, no sounds come out of his mouth when he asks the question.

"What the hell?" Again, no sounds emerge.

"What did you do to me?" Lexicon tries to shout, instead finding that not so much as a whisper worth of sound has left his mouth.

"I can't hear you, Lexicon. And nobody will, for as long as I'm concerned. If you insist on taking words, then I've decided that the best thing I can do is return that courtesy to you by preventing you from having something just as essential: Your sound."

"Prevention, end this!" Lexicon says, unable to come to terms with the fact that he is now inaudible.

"Get used to it. I can keep this going for as long as we live. It's not nearly as taxing as preventing your expression from taking words from everyone in existence."

The word *disintegrate* writes itself across Lexicon's palm, but Prevention interjects, saying: "Don't try it. I can still prevent you from using your expression while keeping you muted. There's nothing you can do to stop me, Lexicon."

Hearing this, Lexicon lunges towards Prevention. Prevention stops Lexicon mid-lunge and moves behind him before unpausing him.

"I didn't say I was done, Lexicon. I'm going to prevent sounds from reaching you too. My voice will be the last thing you ever hear. Prepare to experience absolute silence."

A rift opens beside Lexicon and four letters pour out, spelling the word *wait!*

"Sorry Lexicon, but you brought this on yourself when you thought you could have your way without consequences."

Prevention brings her index finger to her lip and closes her eyes for a second. When she opens them back again one word exits her lips: *done.*

Lexicon sees her speak but can't hear what she has to say. In fact, Lexicon hears nothing at all. He is trapped in localized silence.

I'll gut you. I promise that, Lexicon expresses by summoning more letters.

"If you could hear me, you'd know I'm saying, *so try,* Lexicon."

Lexicon smirks. He summons another torrent of letters that form the sentence: *"I might not be able to hear you. But I still know what words you're using. And I'll do better than try."*

Prevention raises her eyebrows in surprise. Then shakes her head. "You might be able to understand my words, but you've taken them away from every other living thing, so you'll have nothing to know from anyone else. Enjoy the silence you brought on yourself."

A sword of haphazard letters forms in Lexicon's hand which spell out *Die*

Lexicon is rocked back 100 feet. His nose shattered.

"And if you were wondering why my hits on you only ever get harder, there's this funny thing called *stopping power*."

"Take that as a parting gift. I've done what I needed to do. If you insist on keeping words to yourself, I'll ensure you stay muted. I'm leaving now. And I won't let you follow me. I'll be stopping your expression, too."

Digesting Prevention's words, Lexicon thrusts his sword towards her, but fails to make contact. Prevention vanishes as Lexicon shouts in anger, no sound leaving his anguished mouth. He falls to his knees and strikes the ground with his fist, creating a vast crater within. Utterly soundless, Lexicon grits his teeth in silence before a swirling rift opens up in front of him. He walks through seamlessly to the wordscape beyond, his fist clenched hard enough to draw blood.

It's one thing to get muted, it's another for an embodiment to lose their expression. Words come crashing through the sky like lightning, others like rain, the teardrops of Lexicon's pain. For even without the use of his expression the wordscape still responds to Lexicon's will, this being the world he emerged from and built word by word. He may not be able to wield words as he had done prior, but some roles he plays as the embodiment of words still remain. The ground of words Lexicon walks on molds itself into the air like a staircase in the direction of a mountain of words.

Lexicon is smothered by the silence. Even the wordscape naturally produces sound, but Lexicon is unable to hear any of it. He knows every word that exists in this realm and yet the domain feels alien in its cryptic silence. Shaking his head low as he walks, he can't let the silence psych him out. At least he still has words. Yes, with those still safely in his hands, he can handle this strife, or any. Reaching the top of the mountain one outstanding thought crosses his mind: *what if I were to take words away from the embodiments.* Even Prevention couldn't prevent that.

It has become clear to Lexicon that the embodiments have already connived about him and his machinations. And that talk between them is what has brought so much resistance to Lexicon against his taking of words.

So, he decides, in order to preserve what semblance of peace he still has, he will take words from them so they can't plot their resistance further. Besides, all of the embodiments Lexicon had met since his rebellion have never seen the actual merit in Lexicon's ownership of said words.. Since that was the case, then they didn't deserve words anyway; since that was how they wanted to handle things, then they could find a new way to communicate with one another. It wasn't Lexicon's problem if they couldn't. With that he clasps his hands and upon separating them, all words are ripped from existence, for humans and embodiments alike.

There is only one embodiment who will still have the power of speech, however, and that knowledge rumbles the wordscape with Lexicon's rage.

The word *Prevention* is formed from letters which soar beside their master, and Lexicon clasps the word before crushing it into a fine powder. He convulses in anger but remembers one thing: The prevention of words taxes Prevention heavily. She won't be able to avert more than herself and a few other living beings from having their words taken without straining herself too severely. It is a shallow victory, but one all the same for Lexicon. Prevention will have to suffer living in a world where nobody else uses words, or even understands what the words being spoken are, leaving her unable to put her own to use. It is enough to quell Lexicon's rage for the time being.

He sits on a bench of letters at the summit of the word-mountain, and in front of him a familiar anvil forms. Lifting his arm, letters swarm to his hand and he strikes them down with the force of a cannon. With each strike, letters slowly rise into the air and bind together to form new sounds and syllables of Lexicon's making. This time no satisfying clangs accompany the creation of each word. *Vungen,* the new word spells. It is a word Lexicon creates emotionally, not rationally, which conveys the complicated feeling he experiences, having had himself muted and his expression stopped after doing something he only felt was right. For even if *injustice* could just as easily replace his choice of word, something about Prevention's method of retaliation told him that word wouldn't quite fit.

The silence and dissatisfaction from his inability to hear and feel the results of his craft boils within him. Anger, frustration, and sorrow eat away at his vocabularic soul, his loss comparable to a linguist trapped in a room with circus animals. What's the point? The process of making words feel different, incomplete, for the silent clangs of his hammer reap no subsequent fruit of labor.

Now frustrated, Lexicon throws his hammer to the ground and stands up in agitation. Looking down at the tool he just discarded, a pang of self-consciousness hits Lexicon as a reaction to his aggressive behavior.

"I need to cool off," he says, only the words can't audibly emerge. He clenches his fist and a rift opens up in front of him as silently, he enters.

Lexicon comes out of the other side of the rift greeted by the expanse of a jungle, complete with canopies of trees and a jungle floor sprawling with plant-life. He walks along brushing aside the thick foliage of shrubbery until he arrives at his intended destination. In front of him, a waterfall gushes down onto the rocks of a large pool which Lexicon stands at the bottom of, his feet inches from the water. Coming here, Lexicon hopes he can find some relief from the tension he has built up since having himself muted and blocked from hearing. The sight of the waterfall is a natural wonder, one which Lexicon has come to appreciate since he arrived on Earth. Such a sight as always succeeded in his eventual tranquility.

Staring at the waterfall now however, Lexicon is only made painfully aware of how different the experience of watching it without being able to hear the sounds it produces. The view is stunning but looking at it now, Lexicon realizes just how much he valued the other senses he once had. While the sight of the water falling always left him in awe, it was the sound of it crashing down onto the rocks that quelled any murmurs of tension and stress Lexicon had, for it was the combination of both which mesmerized him.

Lexicon is tackled to the ground by an undetected attacker! Looming over Lexicon is a black jaguar, its massive paws pinning him to the jungle floor. Fangs bared the animal thrusts toward the throat of its prey, yet its teeth don't break flesh. Lexicon thrusts upward and the beast is thrown upward, tumbling through the air but landing seamlessly on all four paws. The jaguar slides against the soft, muddy soil and meets the trunk of a tree with a sharp thud.

Lexicon stands and turns to face his attacker. It has assumed a low-stance, ready to pounce at Lexicon at a moment's chance. Lunging toward Lexicon with claws extended, the embodiment lodges himself under the cat and uses the momentum of the lunge to throw the creature into the crystal clear pool below the waterfall. Before the jaguar can recollect itself to continue its assault, Lexicon opens a rift back to the wordscape and jumps through , the rift quickly closing behind him. He has no qualms with creatures who haven't scorned words.

Returning to the word mountain he was at before, Lexicon clasps his neck. If that jaguar had been more dangerous he could've lost his life right then and there. It was clear that his inability to detect what was around him was not only a huge problem but also somewhat of a sentencing.

Lexicon would go on to spend the next two days exiting the wordscape to seek out stimulation which could fill the hole he was beginning to feel. Little made him feel better. Nothing made him feel more comfortable living in this artificial silence imposed on him. Lexicon only grew more bitter as his feelings became more conflicted as the hours passed.

From somewhere, both invisible and soundless, keeping a good eye on him all the same, Prevention receives a mental message from Thought: *"Dictionary is coming. Show her the way to Lexicon, will you?"*

Prevention obliges, happily.

IT HAPPENS while Lexicon is standing alone at the edge of the ocean of a secluded beach, its waves crashing like steady breaths in and out over the sand. In the sight of broad daylight, coming down from the sky; a planetoid– composed entirely of papyrus, stops above the water in front of Lexicon. A seven-foot tall figure descends from the planetoid, carried by sheets of paper until they stand face to face with Lexicon on the sand of the beach.

"Lexicon, I presume?" the figure calls out to him.

Lexicon's brow furrows. Beside him, a rift opens up and letters pour out of it, forming a sentence.

How do you know me? And how are you using words? the sentence spells out. Behind them, a face tired of fighting.

"I know of all embodiments, Lexicon. And I use words because I want to. You may be able to take them away from other existences, but you won't be able to do that to me."

"I go by List. Some call me Dictionary. And just as you embody the concept of words, I embody the concept of where those words are collected. I am the chronicler of words."

Lexicon's eyes widen.

With the rift still open, a further stream of letters pours out, forming Lexicon's next sentence, *Another embodiment who deals in words... I didn't know that was possible.*

"I was the first embodiment to deal in words, Lexicon."

You came before me? How can I know that's true? the letters spell out.

"Before one has a lexicon of words to use, there needs to be a list of words to choose from. That's what a dictionary is: the place words are stored before one can build their own lexicon from it. I hold a record of every word, I know their meanings. And I know when those words become personified by emerging embodiments. Before words even existed, I existed to store them. When enough words were made, you emerged to embody them. And when that day came, I chronicled your existence in my ledger, too." List says, as she outstretches her palm to summon a page from the planetoid, handing it to Lexicon.

"See for yourself if you'd like."

Looking at the page, Lexicon reads a description of himself that he has never told another living being. It reads: "Lexicon: Tenth to emerge. The embodiment of words. Within him resides every letter to create any words he may so choose. He may wield words as he chooses."

"You took the role of making words away from their original creators, the humans. But all the same, I have continued to store those words and their meanings made by you in my ledger."

To what end? Lexicon lets the letters spell

"For the sake of keeping record of existence's growth, as embodiments emerge to personify the concepts those words describe. If any embodiment requires insight as to what their place in existence is, Me and my ledger will be there to enlighten them."

That's nice, but what does that have to do with me?

Just as List is about to answer, a growing sound of beating air begins to fill the vicinity.

"What is that?" List asks, as the sound grows unbearably louder with every passing moment.

What's what? You still haven't answered my question, Lexicon retorts.

"You can't hear that? It's louder than me!" List shouts, trying to raise her voice over the now near deafening sound of air being beaten against wind.

For a moment Lexicon stands stagnant, not a letter coming out of the rift besides him. Visible vungen on his face.

Not anymore, the letters finally come out.

List tilts her head to the side and looks at Lexicon, confused.

"If you can't hear that, how can you hear me?" she asks.

I can't, Lexicon replies.

List's eyes widen as she looks behind Lexicon, seeing the source of the deafening sound making its way towards the two embodiments from the sky.

List points towards the object. Lexicon turns to face it.

The rift releases more characters which spell out the word *helicopter.*

"I have record of that word, I know its definition. I've never seen one before, though. And I didn't expect them to be so loud," List says to Lexicon, who is still turned to face the mechanical marvel.

He turns back and looks at her.

Have you ever seen one before? His letters spell out.

"I just told you... Wait. If you can't hear me, you've been reading the words off of my mouth this entire time, haven't you?"

How perceptive of you, he acknowledges.

"That helicopter is still approaching us. It would be best

if we aren't seen. You know how to conceal your physical form by becoming purely conceptual, yes?"

Learning to manifest a physical form outside of the conceptual plane was one of the first lessons I had to teach myself. Of course I can still do it, Lexicon allows the letters to spell out.

"Then make haste and conceal yourself," List says, turning her form conceptual.

Fine. The less interaction with humans, the better, Lexicon's words spell out, as he makes himself conceptual too.

"I can't conceal the ledger of words though. If the helicopter takes interest in that, it won't leave us alone," she says, pointing towards the floating mass of paper-like pages which carried her here.

"Come with me, Lexicon. You wanted to know why I came here– we have some things to discuss. Important things."

Lexicon looks at List with a reluctance that softens to neutrality.

If only because you're an embodiment of words, too, Lexicon's letters spell out.

"Good. Brace yourself, this may become turbulent," List says as the pages of the massive planetoid swarm down and envelop both embodiments. It carries them off into the air and ascends past the Earth's upper atmosphere, stopping their ascent when they reach low orbit.

"We can talk here," List says.

Alright. Spit it out then, Lexicon allows his letters to spell.

"First, I must know why you insist on using letters to speak for you. Does this have something to do with you not being able to hear?"

Lexicon clenches his fist. The question alone vexes him.

My sound was taken from me. Both my ability to produce it and my ability to receive it. Using my letters is the only way I can still communicate, Lexicon replies.

"What a harsh thing to do to someone. Who would do such a thing to you?"

"Another one of our race. The embodiment called Prevention," Lexicon spells.

"An embodiment named Prevention?" List asks, as the pages of her paper-like world shuffle all around them, each page appearing in front of List as it carries the name of an embodiment.

"Inconceivable. I don't have any record of a Prevention. My ledger updates itself every time a new embodiment emerges. That is my expression. This 'Prevention' shouldn't have emerged yet if they aren't in my ledger," she says.

"I can assure you, the way she fought, Prevention must've been emerged for some time now," Lexicon says, his fist still clenched in anger.

Studying Lexicon's face, List notices the slight displacement of Lexicon's nasal-bridge

"Some time... *Time*... That bastard. This is his doing. Prevention must be an embodiment from the future. So that's who that little narc was. She found me on the outskirts of this solar system. All she told me was that it was in my best interest to believe her about your whereabouts. I knew she was an embodiment, but she disappeared before I had the time to understand her."

From the future? She said he came to stop me.

List's expression turns serious.

"Stop you from what?" she asks, wanting to hear it from the man himself.

"I think you know."

List sighs a long breath.

"Time does only do this kind of thing when it's necessary."

Necessary? Lexicon asks through letters, the offense written on his face.

"Because you're putting existence in jeopardy, Lexicon. That's why I'm here."

No. I'm not doing this again, Lexicon lets his letters spell.

"Doing what?"

Having this same debate with another embodiment about my own right.

"Don't forget Lexicon, I'm just as much of an embodiment of words as you are. Can you be sure this will be the same debate as any of the others you've had?" List asks.

Lexicon stands motionless in argument with himself over what to do next. Finally, he summons the letters to say:

Humanity had their chance to use words. I watched them for millennia as they abused words, defiled them, and turned them into tools meant to control and subjugate each other. At some point, I had to step up in my role as the embodiment of words and change that. You know the definition of all words, correct? Then you must know of the numerous vile and hateful words humanity has come up with to describe one another. I refuse to even utter the slurs.

"I am aware of those words and the... depth of their meaning. I hear you well, Lexicon."

Then you agree that humanity has lost their right to use them?

"I understand why you would feel they have. But what of the rest of existence that you've taken words from?"

If the creators of words went astray in their usage, then it would've only been a matter of time before other races of existence began abusing the languages they stumbled upon. I could remove the hateful words from their lexicons, but then I would be controlling their language. That has never been my intent. At the same time, it is my responsibility to keep language at a certain standard. By taking words away completely from those existences early, I gave them the chance to come up with something of their own accord to utilize that they can tarnish without blemishing words any further.

"You don't find that preemptive judgment authoritarian in its own right? You are preventing whole civilizations from ever having the chance to evolve their usage of words, based on the crimes of Earth."

I'm not dictating how they should live their lives. I'm simply preventing them from becoming another species who use a medium like language to spread hate.

"Many will die because they've lost their means to communicate," List says.

I have already seen many die when propaganda fueled by hateful, weaponized words sway whole populaces into either joining despicable regimes or turning a blind eye to them. I refuse to allow any other races to follow. Those who survive without words will find something new to express themselves with. Perhaps they will use that medium more considerately than humans have.

"I find your stance misguided. I have a record of every word ever made. That includes the words made before you emerged to start creating them. As much as humanity has brought hatred into this world using words, they have also brought good. Words they created like *beauty*, *love*, and *virtue* that exude radiance and give way to joy and happiness. Do you simply ignore what good they and other races can produce when allowed to express themselves, even in spite of their follies?"

Lexicon stares at List after reading the words off of her lips. He's had numerous arguments with embodiments about his taking of words by now, but none before like this.

It simply isn't enough for me to turn a blind eye to the hatred they spread in their usage of words. You say they created good with words like virtue. I've watched senseless crusades waged in that very name, Lexicon counters.

"Hate exists. That's an undeniable fact. And as much as you despise words being used to express that hate, you need to realize that taking words away from anyone who could use them is simply running away from facing that hate. It still exists, whether in word form or not. By allowing races to use words, you create the opportunity for those races to use words in rejection of hate— words of good. You allow them to express themselves freely in the medium that best conveys the nuance of their feelings. Those feelings contain just as much good as the bad you despise," List gently returns.

Words of malistic purpose existing at all are already more than I am willing to bear. Words weren't made to spread hate, Lexicon argues.

"You're right that words weren't made to spread hate. Words were made to communicate with and, they grow based on their interactions with one another. Those interactions are facilitated by the communication between word users who shift and change word meanings and usages as they utilize them. By taking words away from everyone in existence, don't you see that you are constricting words themselves, limiting them to only what you define? You think you're protecting words by taking them away from those who defile them, but really, you're removing an essential aspect of what makes words valuable in the first place, that is; their capacity to share language between existences. You may develop new words, but the way those words evolve in their usage is determined by those who end up using them. Without anyone but yourself to use words, words themselves will only exist in a vacuum, becoming a dead medium altogether. I find that prospect much worse than a sub-section of word-users using language to spread hate, when I know that an equal number of word-users could be using language to spread good."

It won't be a dead medium because you'll still have some words too, he maintains.

"Not for your lack of trying to take those words from even me. What of the rest of our kind?"

None of the embodiments I encountered understood why I was taking words away from existence, or maybe they didn't want to. In fact, they began plotting with each other over my actions which only brought unnecessary conflict to me for a decision I was within my right to make. Embodiments lost their right to have words when they decided to challenge my decision as the embodiment of words.

"You've allowed your role as the embodiment of words to blind you, Lexicon. Don't you realize what taking words from embodiments does?"

I am aware.

"All because they don't agree with your crusade? Protecting words, while sentencing existence to its end, is quite the short-sighted decision, no?"

My hand was forced.

"You forced your own hand when you decided to play judge by sentencing existence to a wordless fate in the first place."

Existences don't need words the way I do. They can find something new, but I will always be the embodiment of words. Words are all I have. That's why keeping them pristine is so important to me. You should understand, as another embodiment of the same keeping.

"I understand the value of words, Lexicon. Perhaps you are still too young to."

And what do you mean by that? Lexicon asks, insulted by the suggestion.

"You had your sound taken from you, yes? How does that make you feel?"

How is that relevant?

"If you answer my question, maybe you can find out."

It's frustrating. Not being able to make a sound. Not being able to hear anything. As if I have been partly removed from interacting with the world.

"Vungen?" List inquires, staring straight into Lexicon's eyes.

You really do know every word. Yes, vungen

"The word you're trying to avoid by creating that is *regret*, Lexicon."

"You are aware of the word *deaf*, correct?" List continues.

"Of course I am. It describes those who are audibly limited."

"Good. Deaf people, unlike yourself, did not bring their inability to hear onto themselves. It is simply a condition they have to live with."

I don't see where you're going with this.

"Perhaps some deaf people feel tormented due to their condition, but they still find ways to overcome their disability. You are able to read the words off of my lips and in turn you and can project words to communicate. Deaf people learn to communicate using words through sign-language. Don't you see? Deaf people, through their ingenuity and determination, found a way to use words just so they can participate in the world. The same world you say you feel partly removed from. It is you who took that ability to participate away from them when you took words. You feel *vungen* for being sentenced to a world without sound, yet you imposed that same sentence on those who overcame their soundlessness just to speak."

"I–I hadn't thought about them when I took words."

"You haven't been thinking about anyone but yourself. Words connect people, bring them together, and provide the means through which they are able to communicate. Despite harm coming from some people's use of words, in the case of deaf people, they need them to communicate through their condition. What use do words have if they aren't being used? Hoarding them to yourself is only keeping them from being used to their fullest potential," she says, exasperated.

And you think that fullest potential includes the hate speech word-users have spread?

"I can't pretend those hateful words have any use beyond spreading pain. What I do know is that those hateful words are outnumbered by countless better ones, not to mention helping the emergence of embodiments who personify what those words encapsulate conceptually. Humans are the ones who came up with words, and still today, they give words new meaning through their use of them. They may still come up with words of hate despite your best wishes, but all the same, there will always be the chance that they come up with something better. You may develop most of the new words now, but every once in a while, a human may come along who stumbles upon a new term of their own, based on the letters you have stored inside of you."

With me here there shouldn't ever be a need for humans or anyone else to come up with new words. That's my role now.

"Look, Lexicon. Prevention took your sound for a reason. Perhaps that reason was to make you realize what it is like to live without something you find essential. Existences may not need to be the prime maker of words anymore, but that doesn't make words any less integral to their way of life. Humanity creates dictionaries of their own. That doesn't reduce me in my role as the chronicler of words. I still have my role to play. You have to stop seeing word-users as a threat to words, when they are merely practitioners of a medium still finding its way. They will never embody words the way you or I do, but that doesn't stop them from inno-vating with words when they are at their best. They might never learn to appreciate words in the same way you do, but removing their chance to ever try isn't justice; rather, it is only its own form of hate."

Lexicon turns to face the Earth beneath them. His eyes shift from continent to continent of the planet, as he thinks about the lives of every person he's taken words from. He thinks about the many embodiments who had come to him to plead he act otherwise. He thinks about words, their place in existence, and his role as the embodiment of them. Waves of contemplation wash over his face. His hands clench into fists beside his torso. Quivering silently. For a few moments Lexicon remains like this, fists shaking, as he stares at Earth. Gradually, his fists relax.

So I'm just supposed to give words back? he asks.

"It would be the right thing to do."

And I'm just supposed to hope that existences use them better than they have? I want assurance that things won't be the same this time around.

"I can't give you that, but I know an embodiment who can, if that's what you really want."

Take me to this embodiment.

"That won't be necessary. I assumed you had your reasons for taking words and supposing you agreed to give them back, you'd have terms. I made contact with an embodiment prior to coming here, in hopes a compromise could be found. They're already here."

Then where are they?

"They *prefer* not to be seen unless necessary. Now that it has been established that you two might discuss-"

"I've got it from here, List," a voice beside them calls out.

Lexicon's eyes bulge open in shock as suddenly, as if coming out of camouflage, a human-looking entity steps in front of List and faces Lexicon eye-to-eye. The entity extends its palm towards him.

"Hello Lexicon, I've heard much about you."

Lexicon stares at the entity, frozen in bewilderment, before he lets the first words of his letters spell *I can hear you!*

"I've heard all about how you had your sound taken away. You don't have to worry about that while we talk."

"How?" Lexicon asks, hearing his own voice for the first time in two days. "How are you even talking when I took words away from everyone in existence?"

"To both of your questions: because I *prefer* it that way. Are you really not going to shake my hand?"

"I don't even know who you are," Lexicon rebuts.

"He's off to a pretty bad start. I might start to reconsider my being here if he keeps this up," she says to List.

List replies: "You heard his motivations, too. He might've gone about solving the problem of words being abused the wrong way, but his intentions to protect them were almost admirable."

"That's easy for another embodiment of words to say. I've yet to see if he's really worth entertaining."

"I don't appreciate being spoken about as if I'm not here. Just who are you?" Lexicon asks.

"Didn't you hear List? I'm the embodiment who can give you the insurance you're looking for if you want to protect those words you hold so dear. The name's Preference."

"Preference... How are you supposed to give me that insurance?"

"Because if I prefer things a certain way, I can make that how things are. In other words, getting your insurance just depends on whether or not I prefer things the way you'd like them to be."

"It would be that simple for you?"

"That depends on the preference."

"Just how much of existence is based on your preferences right now?" Lexicon interjects, finding himself on guard.

Preference lets out a belly laugh before answering Lexicon's question.

"Less than you'd imagine. When I emerged, I could barely fathom the fact that my preference for something as simple as a warmer climate, was influencing the world around me. List visited me and explained my expression to me. She taught me control before I altered the universe irreversibly. I owe her for that. Now I'm quite tame with my preferences. Every once in a while though, something or someone, will prompt me to prefer things differently to the way they are," Preference states.

"Today, List had me come here to see whether or not a preference could be found which could alleviate existence of the issue you caused. You could say I'm paying her back for the favor I owe from all of those years ago. Before you get to make a preference for how things should be though, I have to know that you're worth me changing the way I prefer things now. That's my rule."

"And how am I supposed to prove I'm worthy of your prospective change?"

"We talk. I'd prefer if we did that alone, though," Preference says, glancing over to List.

"Wait Prefer, that wasn't the deal."

"Sorry Listy, I prefer doing this part my way."

Preference and Lexicon vanish from the paper-like planetoid holding them in low orbit, leaving List standing alone, with only the Earth in front of her for company.

"That damn embodiment... Good luck Lexicon. I hope you get what you wanted," List says, speaking openly to the space around her.

A moment later, Preference and Lexicon appear at the highest point of a rocky protrusion, so tall that from its top, the two embodiments can see the curvature of the distinctly alien planet they stand atop of. All around them a rust land-scape sprawls all the way to the horizon on every side.

It takes a moment for Lexicon to adjust to the lack of air on the planet, but like all entities of a conceptual constitution, breathing is not a requirement for life.

Lexicon speaks first.

"Where are we?" He asks, finding the sound of his voice much fainter than what he's normally used to.

"Its preferred name is Mars. And this volcano we're standing on goes by Olympus Mons."

"You brought me to Mars? Why here?"

"I said I'd prefer if we spoke alone. As far as I know, there shouldn't be anyone here to disturb our conversation. I didn't want to get too far away from List, though. I'd give her half-an-hour to get here on her ledger once she realizes where we've come to."

"How would she even know?"

"List has a way of tracking down embodiments no matter where they are. This shouldn't take longer than the time it takes for her to reach us, though. That is, if we can get this done quickly. In which case, I suggest you start talking. "

"About what?"

"Your reasoning for taking words."

"I thought you heard everything I said to List."

"I did. But I want your real reason for taking words," Preference says, suddenly becoming more stern than she had been before.

"My real reason? What do you mean? It's like I said, humanity have tarnished words with their usage of them, and so I prevented the rest of existence from doing the same by-"

"If you won't say it, I will. You don't think they're worthy of words the same way you are, do you?"

Lexicon stands quiet as he faces Preference before he replies: *No, I don't.*

"But they were the ones who created words, weren't they?"

"All the same, I was the one to grasp them."

"And how have you done that, really?"

Outstretching his hand, Lexicon allows three symbols to rise from his palm.

"I've tinkered away at the foundation of what makes words what they are. These three glyphs alone will be the basis for thousands of new words in coming time."

"That's good and all, but aren't you going to be the only one who can use them if words are taken from everyone else?"

"My first intention was only ever to create words. Taking them away was my reaction to the vile usage I saw in my time on Earth."

"I hear you talk, and all I get is the sense that you ooze self-righteousness," Preference informs him.

"Excuse me?"

"You really think that just because some people use words in a way you deem incorrect, you get to take them away from everyone in existence?"

"I emerged as the sole conductor of words. If you were given my capacity to oversee words, and encountered their abuse, wouldn't you do what you felt was necessary to protect them? I've simply been fulfilling my role up until now."

"Don't misunderstand me, Lexicon. I get it. Words are your domain and as such you feel responsible for them. You feel it's your duty to do right by them, no matter what it takes. Where you've gone wrong however, is thinking that just because you hold authority over words, you're free to do something as significant as take them away without any repercussions. Especially, when you're taking them away from embodiments too," she adds.

"I'm the embodiment of preferences. I emerged with the capacity to alter existence based on my preferences, and based on the preferences of anyone else I agree or disagree with. Since I learnt to control my expression, I've been able to sense the preferences of every being in the galaxy. You feel existence lost its right to have words when they started abusing them? Think about the preferences I must have heard over the course of my lifetime. You blame the humans for your taking of words? I've heard the preferences from members of their race who want nothing more than to exterminate members of their own species for something as insignificant as their skin, beliefs, or gender. I've heard the preferences of those in power to keep their populaces controlled by the few instead of by the many. I've heard preferences for profit over the protection of nature. Through all of this, don't you think I considered playing the same role as you do now? As an enforcer of how I preferred things to be?" she concludes.

"You get it." Lexicon says, his chest emptying of all tension.

"If I had my preference back then, there would be no nobody carrying any of those hateful preferences now. It would've been as simple as preferring the next global virus afflicted only those I deemed had the wrong preferences."

"Why didn't you?"

"I realized that even though it was my place to influence how my, or other preferences altered existence around me, doing something as drastic as eliminating all those I found unsavory would be stripping existence of individuality and choice. That would bend the universe to my image, and I don't own such authority. The longer I heard their preferences, the more I came to understand that all of those hateful desires were countered by just as many good-natured ones who desired peace, unity, and safety. It was then that I knew my role wouldn't be to decide *whose* preferences I deemed worthy, but to alter existence when I deemed a preference worthy of implementation. It's a subtle change, but one that made all the difference in my continuance as the embodiment of preferences. It allows individuality of preference to exist, while I still play my role justifiably."

Listening to Preference, Lexicon looks down at his hands in silence. He brings them to his face before shaking his head in disappointment.

"I've been going about this the wrong way, haven't I?" he admits as words run in a stream of tears down his solemn cheeks.

Preference stands there looking at him.

"Yes, you have."

"I've been imposing my will instead of finding a way to resolve the issue."

"Yes. But, I had to have List teach me control. I suspect you didn't have the same kind of mentorship to teach you the difference between your authority and the moral considerations in your role as the embodiment and overseer of language."

"I understand. Words were made for everyone to use before me, and they should be for everyone to use now. I'll return words to existence. I can find a way to improve their usage without taking them away. That's all I ever wanted to do."

"Now you're sounding rational. I like it. You wanted insurance that words wouldn't be abused in the same way, I can give that to you now. You've self-reflected and grown. You've earned the right to make a preference in my book."

"For simply realizing my mistake?"

"For reminding me of myself when I started pondering how far I could go in my role as the overseer of a concept, and choosing the path of free expression. Plus, it's like I said, I owed List for what she did for me. Consider this me doing the same thing for you: giving you a chance to make things the way you want without taking away the individuality of those around you."

"Thank you."

"Now, state your preference. How would you rather things be to ensure your words are more protected than they were before?"

"I have to think about this."

"Go ahead. We still have about 20 minutes before Dictionary gets here."

"Alright. I need to be alone for this."

"Fine by me. I'll come back when you're ready."

"Where will you go in the meantime?"

"Sightseeing. I haven't been in the Solar System in centuries. I'm going to check out Jupiter," she grins.

"Ok. How will you know when I'm ready?"

"I'll know you have a preference. It's as simple as that. Be quick. I want to get this done before List gets here."

"I'll try."

"That's good enough for me. See ya!" Preference says to Lexicon before she vanishes, preferring herself on Europa, Jupiter's icy moon.

Lexicon stands alone on Olympus Mons and before long, sits down to consider all he has been through these past few weeks. He thinks about Freedom who he trapped just to take the word from humanity. He thinks of Reality, and the furious battle they raged. He thinks about Prevention, who took something of value to him to make Lexicon understand what it felt like to lose something of value; he thinks of his encounters with List and Preference, the two embodiments who finally got through to him with their words alone.

Lexicon thinks about the role he's played so far from the maker of words to the taker of them. How he hadn't felt much happiness in taking words, where he enjoyed every moment of making them. Lexicon thinks of the words he has taken from embodiments and how that decision had put existence in jeopardy. Which he was too stubborn to fully comprehend against his grudge. All he could grasp then was the prospect of living in a world where words were abused. Now, all Lexicon thinks about is the danger he posed to language based on the crimes of humanity. And that's when it clicks for Lexicon, ten minutes after Preference leaves.

Preference suddenly returns to Olympus Mons.

"Cutting it close there Lexicon, aren't you?" she says.

"Yes. But I know what must be done now."

"Well, don't keep me waiting. Let's hear your preference and see if it's something I can get behind. The view was beautiful by the way."

"Words are my responsibility, but in a world where they are integral to more than just me, perhaps it is time those who use them accept their weight as I have. I may be the embodiment of words but as Prevention correctly stated, eventually embodiments emerge to personify specific concepts in a way I can't. It then becomes that embodiment's responsibility to uphold the concept it represents. So, if humanity and other races want to use words, then it's time they accept the same level of responsibility over words that embodiments have to."

"I'm interested. Go on."

"Embodiments will continue to emerge for as long as there are concepts to personify, but I would prefer if the way that happened changed. If a human or any other existence already personifies a word in the way they live their life, then it wouldn't be right for existence to have to wait for an embodiment to emerge to personify that word's concept. No, that human or other being should be the one to fill that role and bear the weight of that responsibility."

"Say it clearly."

"I want the beings living here and now, who already personify everything the word defines, to become that concept's embodiment. If existences want to use words, then we'll see how existence fares when the responsibility to uphold concepts is theirs to carry. I'll keep making letters and words, but I'll let existences come up with their own too, and those who embody those concepts will uphold them. I only ever wanted what was fair. Sharing the responsibility of words with those who wish to use them means that if they abuse words now, then they'll be abusing existence themselves. That will be my insurance; the fact that now existences will shoulder the same responsibility to treat words with respect as I do. That's the fairest solution I can imagine without taking words away from existence. That is my preference. That is what I want."

"As you wish," Preference says. "That's quite the tall order you ask of me. Your preference will fundamentally change the way embodiments exist in this world. I won't be able to make another preference as large as that for the next few hundred years. But, it does make sense. Since only humans have advanced enough to make use of the majority of words in existence, are you okay with them starting out as the new embodiments who emerge?"

"That works for me. Multiple embodiments I met defended the humans. Now we'll see if the humans were worth that protection when they're the ones embodying concepts in the same way we do now."

"Irony, I like it. They won't really be human anymore,

though. They'll be shedding their humanity in becoming conceptual. They'll be no different than any of us."

"That works for me. As long as you can fulfill this preference."

"I plan to, though we should probably consult List for this. I don't see why she wouldn't agree though, her role as the chronicler of words and emerging embodiments will stay relatively the same. All that's left now then, is for you to return words to existence."

"Yes. I think it's about time I did that," Lexicon says, holding his hand above his head. A bottomless flood of words exits Lexicon's palm and escapes into space. Within minutes, the words touch down on Earth, entering humans as they go about their apocalypse. With every word that enters a person, they gain the ability to use language again. All around the universe words return to existences who use them through rifts, just in time for List to reach Mars.

"Lexicon, I take it those words came from you?" List says as she lands beside them both.

"Yes, I'm returning what I've taken. They won't be able to see these words, but once they're touched by them, they should have everything returned to them."

"Good. I take it you got your insurance, then?"

"About that, we have some stuff to tell you about Lexicon's preference, Listy. I think you'll like it. Before that though, I can stop preferring you to have your sound, Lexicon," Preference turns to him and says.

"Prevention kept her word," Lexicon says, finally having his sound back without the influence of another embodiment...

———————

 the region between Somewhere and Nowhere, talking.

"It looks like he returned words to everyone," Prevention says.

"It does seem that way. They'll be doing much more than that shortly," Time replies.

"Is it anything I should be worried about?" Prevention asks

"Not explicitly. I think we can allow time to run its course from here," Time says.

"So what now?" Prevention asks once more.

"You return to your time, if you'd like."

"How different will it be?"

"For starters, you'll find existence to be much more free than it was before we arrived in the past. Second, it's a lot more interesting of a place embodiment-wise. The rest, you will have to just see for yourself.

"That sounds good to me. Ok. I'm ready to go back. Will I see you when I arrive?"

"Time waits for no-one. But I can spare a moment for a friend," Time says.

"That works!. Goodbye for now, and see you in the future. Don't forget about me by then," Prevention says.

Out of Time's palm a stream of *future* envelops Prevention like a cloud.

As Prevention slowly dissipates, Time tells her: "Foolish P, I always remember," with a smile.

At the same moment, against the backdrop of Olympus Mons, List says, "Alright. Let me hear it. What was your preference?"

Lexicon and Preference smile.

"AND THAT'S the story of how an embodiment threatened existence in his rage, and the measures taken to stop him. They call it *The Lexicon Saga.*"

Answer stares at me silently. Her piercingly blue eyes give away no emotion, which is uncharacteristic for her. I know she had been listening attentively to the story based on her occasional brow-raise or widening eyes, but now that I was done talking, the stillness in her living room felt palpable. Maybe these were just nerves of anticipation I was feeling? It had been a long time since I'd felt anything so... Human.

"Is that your answer then, Endless?" She finally asks, still emotionless behind her youthful voice.

"It is," I reply.

No better answer had come to mind. Besides, I had in fact found the story quite affecting when Ratio relayed it to me. If anything was going to move Answer enough for her to consider teaching me, this was it.

"As far as stories go, that was quite dramatic..." Answer says.

On that, we could agree. Still, that didn't tell me whether or not it was good enough for her approval.

"But if that's going to be your answer, I need something more specific regarding the answer I can actually judge."

I guess not. Not yet anyway.

"I understand. What are you looking for in particular?" I ask.

"Answers are meant to enlighten. One should learn something from any given answer. At this point, you've given me a story. Stories can serve many purposes: entertainment, warnings, or escape. But what about the story you've told me serves as your answer? If this story is an answer, what can it teach me?"

It's my turn for silence now. Grabbing a hold of the hand-made mug Answer had given me hours before, I take my last sip of the green-liquid making up its contents. It's flavor is still unplaceable, but I've actually grown quite fond of the substance. If ambrosia existed, I'm pretty sure it'd taste like the opposite of this stuff. She wants a specific answer. Something that can enlighten her in some way. I use the moment to think. There's only one answer based on that story that comes to mind. At least for me.

Ratio hadn't told me this himself, some part of me just knew— that while Ratio was once *obsessed* with deducing my ratio and others to defeat me and prove his superiority, it was in hearing Lexicon's story, and learning how uncaring Lexicon became to his action's risks on the stability of existence all for the sake of single-mindedly trying to uphold words the only way he had considered how to, that Ratio realized what I was now about to tell Answer.

"The answer here is to the question of purpose. Lexicon felt bound by his purpose, enough that he was willing to jeopardize existence to uphold it. Preference taught him another way. Preference taught Lexicon he didn't have to see his purpose as an immutable law. She taught Lexicon there was always a choice. The decision to do things differently. For a race like ours, I've realized that being bound to a specific purpose as the embodiment of a specific concept seems only natural," I explain.

"The lesson within the Lexicon Saga is quite simple actually: if you allow yourself to become *consumed* by what you believe to be your purpose, that obsession is as harmful as it is intoxicating. Embodiments don't have to be slaves to the concepts they embody. We may have inclinations spurred by our composition, but that does not make us subservient to them. That's my answer; instead of letting one idealized purpose define us, we can decide how to define and redefine that purpose for ourselves."

"Hm. Deciding our own purpose..." Answer trails, a twinge of questioning to her voice.

"Not blind devotion to an unalterable pursuit, a single way of doing things, but rather the autonomy to adapt and change what we live for..." Answer resumes.

"The autonomy to choose how we decide to live at all" I say, my gaze meeting hers.

"You believe we have that choice, even as the concepts we each embody are predetermined?" Answer asks.

"It's not something I have to believe."

"That's how you live?"

"You already know the answer to that don't you?"

A slight smirk works its way onto the Answer's face.

"Yes. But I would've liked to hear you say it."

"I find. I roam. I chase."

"Is that your purpose?" She asks. She can't hide the look in her eyes. Maybe she doesn't want to. Either way, the interest I see written across her gaze is like nothing I've seen from her before. She isn't accessing this answer. She really wants to hear this from me. At that moment, I think I truly understand why she came to Else. This will be the closest I come to understanding why she came here, anyway. She doesn't get to learn much. It's an aspect of living one could easily take for granted. She simply doesn't have that luxury since it's ingrained in her to already *know*. When the opportunity came along to be somewhere she couldn't just have a straight answer to, she jumped at the chance. Right now, she's asking me the subjective question of whether what I do is my purpose?

Answer knows that if she really wanted to, she could ascertain my answer before I even gave it to her. But the nature of the question itself could prompt a *no* as invariably as it could prompt a *yes*. It all hinges on subjective reasoning– that's the line that blurs all definitive answers. Subjectivity. For the first time since she arrived at Else, I might've just put Answer at the edge of her seat. It's then I realize that since she decided to come here, Answer has been deciding how she wants to live her life all along. I haven't known her for very long, but I could imagine that her innate inclination, what she could've seen as her purpose, had to do with ascertaining and coming up with answers.

Yet here she was sitting in front of me, asking questions that didn't have a predetermined answer. Maybe those were the answers she tried to glean now. Maybe she'd been deciding her own purpose all along. After all, it has now been a few seconds of silence since she asked me the question. What I say in reply is as much of an answer for me as it may not be for her. I won't keep her waiting any longer. So, I tell her.

"I just... Keep going."

"... Okay." She says, her illustrious smile emerging for the first time since I started telling the story.

"Your true answer– I find it satisfactory. The direction of

our lives being malleable through our own choice. I quite like that."

"I'm glad you do. I was told this was *a story every embodiment should hear*, and I think it does a good job of getting that answer across."

"But you've known that answer for much longer, haven't you?" Answer says, the tone of her voice telling me she's not really asking me the question.

"I've had a lot of time to."

"So have I. The notion is oh so very *human in origin*, isn't it?" She says, with a wink.

There was no point in hiding anything from her. If it was good enough to be considered a question, she no doubt already had its answer.

"It's been a long time since I could call myself *human*," I say. I could never forget those days of conflict I experienced during my awakening when I became an embodiment. Ratio and I knew those days all too well.

"Don't worry. Neither of us have to speak about those days," she says, sticking her tongue out at me. There's something in that statement, *neither of us*. There is something in that warm playfulness... for a second it almost feels... familiar. As if we've-

"Nevertheless, thank you for indulging me with your answer. You pass, Endless!" Answer says, the delight in her voice tangible.

That's a relief. I spent hours telling her this answer.

"You don't need to thank me for giving you an answer when it was your one requirement of me." I say.

"Of course I do! At least when the answer's good."

"Alright. So what now?"

"Now, we-"

Suddenly, there is a rumbling. A deep, guttural rumbling, that shakes Answer's living room and subsequently her entire house violently, down to the oddly deliquescent yet somehow solid floor. We hold onto our seats trying not to flail helplessly.

"It's happening!" Answer shouts, only excitement oozing from her voice which confuses me, given the predicament.

"What is?" I shout back, trying to raise my voice over the sound of the vicinity's violent thrashing

"Else is going through its shifts!" Answer cries out, a beaming smile spreading across her face.

Ah, she did say something about Else's 'shifts' earlier, didn't she?

Answer stands up and shouts "Come on, follow me!"

So I do.

We make it outside just in time to see our surroundings *unravel* right before our eyes. Looking up, I see the spot where Answer and I came from when we descended towards her house, as the unlacing of everything around us propagates. With every passing moment more of Else is revealed, as its layers deconstruct continuously. For as far as I can see, every iota of our surroundings separate. The turf beneath us *comes undone* as Answer and I begin to spiral downwards. I grab her as we fall beside each other, and I soar. I take us right back to Answer's house, which has begun to crumble and break apart without the support of an *under*. I carry us closer toward the disintegrating edifice that was once her home in a feeble attempt to save it, but Answer whispers *No, let it be.* into my ear. It's unmistakable. She's having fun right now.

"Spin me" She pleads, her arms wrapped around my neck as I hold her waist and we begin rotating in place.

All around us, the unraveling spreads. It's as if our surroundings are being *unwritten*.

"What's going to happen?" I ask.

Answer looks up at me. "I don't know yet. Every shift is

different."

So, this is why she likes them so much. It's a new answer every time.

"Do you know how to dance?" She asks.

And despite the mayhem unfolding around us, I smile. "I know how to try."

"I like it when people try," she says.

We start slowly, my hands still tight around her waist, her arms still around my neck, as we rotate mid-hover. I haven't done this in over a century. Danced. I forgot how... tender it could be. Answer rests her head against my shoulder and whispers *Just watch.*

All around us, our unraveling surroundings break down into their constituent particles. Answer and I find ourselves surrounded by a spectrum of multi-colored particles which take the form of tiny spheres to every direction. The particles flow around us like waves as we dance at the center of it all. It's mesmerizing; the kind of display I know one would have to be lucky to see in their lifetime. Spinning around with Answer as Else swirls, I know I'll cherish it as such.

Answer places her feet on top of mine as we hover, and for someone who hasn't danced in over one-hundred years, I find myself moving in sync with her as I take steps for us, leading our dance. There isn't any music for us to dance to, yet the rhythmic tremble of our surroundings provides us with an unspoken tempo we both instinctively match. Answer unwraps one of her arms from my neck, and with that hand takes one of mine from around her waist and cups our hands. We raise our coupled hands to the side and while I know the concept of age is all but irrelevant to me, I can't help but feel young.

As if I'm back to being the human I once was. My old name, my old life, have long since become distant memories. They aren't who I am anymore. Yet while I dance with her all I can think about are my days on Earth. The family I once had. The friends I'd made. The experiences we shared. Answer brings all of those thoughts back to my mind as we dance. There's something about her. Something I know I recognize.

"You're doing pretty well for just 'trying'" Answer says.

"With you it just comes naturally," I breathe.

"Good answer," she says, pulling her head away from my shoulder to look me in the eyes. She smiles. And for a moment, nothing happening around me is as captivating as the sparks within her's.

"If you keep looking at me like that, you'll miss the show," she laughs.

She's right, so I look back up and around us. I watch as the multi-colored particles begin to oscillate at a singular frequency. A distinct buzzing noise accompanies the vibration. One by one, the particles all around us begin to change color as they vibrate. I notice some particles beginning to pulsate faster than the others; those are the particles that change color first. Those shade-shifting particles continue to oscillate at higher and higher frequencies until they begin to lose their spherical shape and morph into rays of white. The rays shine with a brilliant, pure brightness before streaming from their spot in beams of arcing radiance, leaving no trace whatsoever in their wake.

"They're leaving," I say to Answer, as I watch more and more particles beam away.

It doesn't take long before entire waves of the Else externality eventually leave. Just as suddenly as they arrived...

"Looks like it. Else seems to be *going*," Answer tells me.

I want to ask Answer where, but I already know the answer myself.

"To where areas aren't," I say, completing her sentence.

"Correct. This may be your last chance to follow it if you

want to see it again within the next century. Will you chase it?"

"I came here to find the answer. You're all I'm chasing. So I ask you, will you follow Else?"

"I'd rather have this dance."

"Good answer," I say, smiling. I really like the answer I found.

And so, Else goes as the last remnants of its particles beam away, and I stay, one hand holding Answer's, the other around her waist. I recognize the debris filled surroundings we're now hovering within. After all, I had spent months in it looking for Else. We were back in Elsewhere, the region between Somewhere and Nowhere.

Answer and I push away from each other, our hands still clasped as I twirl her in front of me, and pull her back in. We begin to waltz as we hover, her feet still pressed on top of mine. It's just then that Answer begins to sing.

Her voice isn't angelic or heavenly. In fact, I'd say her singing is quite unrefined. Like she hasn't done it in a long time. All the same, I can't help but enjoy listening to her. It's raw, it's charming. As we dance, I'm completely absorbed by her every word.

Suddenly my eyes widen as the realization occurs that I've heard this song before... it can only be described as *Earthly*. Back when I was human, before I awakened so long ago, I knew a girl. This wasn't any ordinary girl, I recall her going to magnificent lengths just to see or listen to the artist who made the song Answer was now singing. That girl... She had those same piercing blue eyes I saw when I gazed at Answer's face. Even the same voice... my thoughts trail off.

"I know you, don't I?" I whisper into Answer's ear, as she recites the lyrics to John Mayor's "Gravity".

Answer looks up at me and smiles. But the look in her eyes is sad. They're the same sad eyes I saw the only two times she frowned. As if she is reliving a past long since discarded as she stares at me.

"I recognized you from the moment you arrived in Else. You haven't changed much," she admits.

"It really is you... Annalis."

"When you arrived at Else, I quickly realized that you didn't recognize me. So I asked you what your name was. You didn't use your earth name, even though you could've."

"That's not who I am anymore."

"I'm not the girl you remember from all those years back, either. I'm just... Answer now."

"Still, I never thought I'd see you again. How did you come to be Answer?"

"To put it bluntly, a lot happened after you disappeared 80 years ago. Certain people began to exhibit otherworldly capabilities, assuming strange monikers all the while. Most vanished soon after, just like you, while others stayed, performing acts across the globe that defied known limits so much that the world took notice. This emergence became a global mystery. Nobody knew what it meant then, but that didn't stop people from trying to find out. I was one of them. You ask how I came to be Answer? The same way you became Endless,"

I pause as I wait for her to continue.

"Harmonizing with the concept I resonated with, down to a fundamental level. I became dedicated to finding the answer as to why such an explosion of extraordinary beings was occurring. What I knew was that the same namesakes those people gave themselves described their newly gained metaphysical capabilities to the intrinsic level. That's when I realized the answer: those people *embodied* the words they named themselves. Not just exemplified the concepts, but *personified* them down to their very core. Not long after my breakthrough, I began to find the answers for every question that had ever eluded me. In fact, I started finding the answers to the prompts anyone was curious enough to ask. Finally, as eyes began to settle upon me, I was forced to face the question of *what, or who,* I was becoming. And I simply had the answer: I had searched for answers themselves until I became their very embodiment,"she finished with a satisfied smile.

"I only learned those things through my travels." I say.

"Yes, and in them you experienced encounters and learned answers that finally led you down the path to me."

"Is every answer already set in stone?"

"When you look big enough, every phenomenon seems like it leads up to a certain outcome. A mosquito roaming until it finds a home to inhabit, where it proceeds to infect that household's tenant with malaria. If one were to ask the question of whether that tenant would become sick in a week's time, the answer would be a conclusive yes, since the reality is that the event did occur, by the time that week did come around. On a much grander scale, the answer would be set in stone, since the answer, yes, would be confirmed, even if it took the course of a week to solidify. From the tenant's perspective however, through the week, before their biting, every choice they made could lead to a whole different set of possibilities. If they decided to walk instead of drive, they might arrive home much later that night than the mosquito would've been active in their room. And in that sense, until the moment came where they would be bitten by the mosquito, the answer as to whether they would get sick by it, could not be conclusively answered. So, for even as simple of an answer as a yes or no, whether or not that answer was set in stone could not be so simply answered. I find the line between order and chaos in arriving at every answer, whether it is illuminated for me from within, or I decide what it should be. To ask if answers were set in stone would reveal more answers about the nature of existence than the simple yes or no you're looking for."

"You've changed Ann-Answer. You've grown. And yet, you're more you than I ever remember."

"I became exactly what I had become. I could say the same for you, Endless. At least in the time I had come to know you versus now."

"It felt like I just… Awakened. We all did… What's Earth like now?"

"A cacophony of distinct emergences. If I hadn't become so bored of my own existence there, I would still be experiencing wave after wave of new changes the planet is going through."

"Will I ever see it again? Did I lose my family?"

"I've been your friend since the last century was in its infancy. Even without knowing the answers, I know those are really not the kind of answers *you* would want to learn from anybody else but yourself."

"It's just been so long. Seeing you makes me realize how much I've missed it.

"If anybody has the time to revisit it, it's you. We both know that."

"I know. And I plan on making that trip. I just need more time to figure out what my existence means. That's why I came here. For the answer. To learn what I needed to shape the rest of my experience.

"And I'm glad you came. You gave me a new answer to dwell on for the rest of my stay. And you're a friend who I've longed to see for a very long while. I'll take the time to tell you what I know. I can tell you this much: If *figuring* out is what you seek, you won't have to wait long before you find what you want to discover."

"Thank you. I'll take that much. It's really good to see

you again, Answer."

"I could say the same to you, Endless," she says. "Now, set me down on the nearest platform."

So I soar, her hips in my grasp, as we course through the *exception* of Elsewhere, passing by sights that have neither nowhere or somewhere to be. Spirals of blackened smoke hang throughout the expanse. I spot a familiar piece of debris, drifting through the distance at less than miles per hour in what seems like a low gravity state. I land us down onto the same spot.

"This is where I met-"

"Ratio," Answer says. "I always wondered if one could find a way to track Else. That man came frighteningly close. A few more hundred years, and he could produce answers about the nature of existence that even I may pause at. I never got to meet him back on Earth. I always knew he might be an intriguing fellow after you introduced me to his twin. I would've liked to meet him now. Alas, not every one of *our kind* needs to find an answer outside of their own."

"You knew I was searching?"

"I knew someone was coming to visit. It was one of the little prompts I asked of myself a lot since coming to this destination. I left the rest of the answer, that is, of who would be coming to visit, up to *possibility*. I'm glad I did. I am still a fan of a good surprise.

An Answer liking surprises, I couldn't help but chuckle at the notion. We might've changed intrinsically over the course of the last century, but we were still the same kids I remembered us to be, give or take a few incomprehensible experiences. I take a seat in the same spot Ratio had been meditating at when I found him, and beckon Answer to do the same. She gladly complies.

"So, teach me everything," I say.

And so she does.

The story has just begun. Follow Endless across The Labors and find out more in due time.

If you'd like to learn more about my creative endeavors as a whole, allow me to officially introduce you to ExoticCreed!

You can discover the full scope for yourself at https://ExoticCreed.com

I'm also on social media. Chase the stars with me @yugovex on Instagram, (formerly) Twitter, and TikTok

There's still a lot I want to show you all. This is truly the beginning. Thanks for joining the ride.